THE BROMIUS PHENOMENON

THE BROMIUS PHENOMENON

JOHN RANKINE

LONDON: DENNIS DOBSON

First published in Great Britain in 1976
by Dobson Books Ltd,
80 Kensington Church Street, London W8

Printed in Great Britain
by Whitstable Litho Ltd, Whitstable

ISBN 0 234 77073 2

I

There was always work. Rumor had it that it was great therapy.

Senior Controller Dag Fletcher had doubts about that one.

He moved irritably from his desk, crossed his gray wall-to-wall carpet, leaned with both hands flat on the warm glass of his solar window and looked out from his eyrie in the European Space Corporation ziggurat.

Three times he had played a detailed report on his pianola with every refined statistical ploy, and the facts refused to shake down into any kind of pattern.

He told himself he was behaving like an adolescent; that it was flatly against every rule of self-management to emotionalize on experience that was past and gone and that life was one thing after another; that he should duly identify that next thing and leap after it like a hound dog: but it was all for the birds.

The Bromusian Commissar Hulda was still there present in his mind's eye, an unfading eidetic image, eyes warm and affirmative, left side bare to the waist in her people's traditional dress, symbolizing the open heart free from guile.

His sense of loss was greater because he knew that it would finally pass. But reacting to it as of now, he judged that he had used up his ration of sensitivity for the day. To be expected to flip like a twig about the flight schedule of an overdue starship was too much.

On the other hand, it was what he was paid for. The difficult ones stopped at his desk. They had no place else to go.

5

Fletcher's eyes shifted focus and stopped at the glass where his shadowy reflection was superimposed on the backdrop of the terminal complex and the thrusting spires of the ships on their perimeter pads. The broad bands of green and gold on his epaulettes stood out as if shoving forward for recognition. They had been earned, but they needed constant vindication. There were some he had passed in his quick progression from the flight deck to the executive suite who would be glad enough to see him fail.

He was surprised to see his own face, familiar and strangely unfamiliar, hovering over the insignia. It was a lean, hard job, puckered from the left eyebrow by an old radiation burn.

Consideration of it was phased out by an urgent bleep from the clutter of hardware flanking his console. Another face was claiming attention, staring out of the lifesize video screen like a kilogram of mauve putty with the apoplectic glare of one who liked to get what he wanted when he wanted it.

Fletcher eased himself off of his wall and settled in his swivel chair, throwing a switch to put himself in circuit. He said, "Chairman?" in a tone making it clear that, as far as he was concerned, it might just a well have been the lord Krishna coming up for a flute solo.

Paul V. Spencer, all there was of power in the Space Corporation, wasted no words in confirming that it was himself and no doppelgänger. He went straight to the heart of the matter.

"It's eleven o'clock, controller."

There was no point in denying it. The man was right.

"I know it."

"I have one hour before the board meet. I like to

have my facts right. When do I get that report on *Two Nine?*"

"I have nothing to report."

Spencer's face deepened in hue, taxing the color-matching circuitry to its maker's limits, and he appeared to choke a little before he rasped out, "A multibillion dollar starship can fade out on a kindergarten charter in friendly space and I have to tell those political ninny hammers that we have no observations? You know we depend on that committee for finance. God save the mark, do you want them to start an inquiry of their own? They'd like that of course. Just the lever they could use to shove their pig snouts into every department. Neil Walker has a brother in the ministry. There's every kind of pressure on for an explanation. I'll tell you what I can do. I can probably swing it for an adjournment for twenty-four hours. That's the most. I want something definite by eleven hundred hours tomorrow. Now for all our sakes get your finger out."

He ceased and the screen faded to clear silver. Esthetically it was all gain, but the message lingered on.

To be fair, Dag Fletcher reckoned that his chairman had a point. It would give the politicians a field day.

He flicked in the robot secretary and the center of his desk glowed violet, cleared to pale amber and began to display again the blow-by-blow run-down of the history of *Interstellar Two Nine*. Simultaneously its cool electronic voice began to purr out a gloss on the important issues.

No doubt it was all there. Every scrap of information that could be gathered had been lodged in the memory banks, but it was doing nothing for him.

He shoved down the cancellation stud and the voice cut out in midperiod.

Instead, he selected the end switch on the box and summoned his flesh-and-blood help.

When the stainless steel iris eye sliced open and she appeared on the threshold in a black cheong sam with the forked lightning-flash insignia worked in garnets on the collar, he doubted the wisdom. She had not liked Hulda and had made it clear. Relations had been on the cool side in the office.

She said, 'Controller?' much in the way he had said, 'Chairman?' and made no effort to come in.

"Take a seat. I want to talk to you about *Two Nine*."

"Everything we have is on record."

"That I know. But I want to hear it from you."

"The arrangements were made when you were on leave. Controller Fairclough handled the detail." She did not say "Besotted by that blonde Bromusian," but it was there in the small print.

Fletcher said patiently, "Just indulge me, Vanessa, pretend I never heard about it. Tell me all."

"*Interstellar Two Nine* went out thirty days ago just after your leave period started. It was a charter job the details are on the manifest. Commander was Captain Neil Walker whose brother is now pressing for more action."

"On a nice simple charter job for some ethnology outfit."

"That's right. Central Institute of Ethnology. Director Dr. Izod. Headquarters in Brazilia. Financed partly by Earth government and partly by the Inter-Galactic Organization itself. That accounts for the high-level interest. It was an important charter, prestige-wise."

"OK. Get on with the details."

"Dr. Izod was picked up in Fingalna. Then it was a straight run across the Center to Croton."

"Why Croton?"

"That was the destination on the manifest. They were aiming to do some close study of primitives. As I understand it, there is a theory that the Croton people are the same ethnic stock as Bromusians, but it's never been worked out. How it could be, since neither planet had a space fleet before they were discovered by I.G.O. exploration teams."

"An innocent piece of research with no angles."

"So it would appear. But Croton was never reached. The last transmission from Commander Walker came when they had Croton in sight and were leaving the gravisphere of Bromius."

"Bromius Control spoke to them?"

"Of course. Those monkeys never miss a trick."

That was true. Discounting Vanessa's dislike for the people, it was part of their correct and courteous approach. They were a byword for going by the book.

Fletcher shut Hulda out of his mind and harked back to the two visits he had made there. One as an I.G.O. frigate commander on the routine decennial inspection: pointless. There were no offensive weapons to inspect. The people seemed to have eliminated aggression from the national character. They had no space fleet of their own and were content to live a life of gentle and elaborate courtesy in a climate that was a perpetual summer afternoon.

It was a small planet, half the size of Earth, with a controlled population that gave elbow room for civilized living. The crew had been very impressed and if the stay had been longer he reckoned he would have had half the men opting for naturalization. They had left, garlanded with *leis* in a tremendous aura of goodwill. Orchids would still be in orbit where they had been jettisoned out of sight.

The other visit had been in one of the corporation's own freight-and-exploration ships. No change. Medoc, the head man, had gone out of his way to lay on a nonstop entertainment.

"So what followed?"

"Nothing followed. Commander Walker set up the course for a proving orbit around Croton. He spoke to Croton control and they checked his plot. It was OK. He acknowledged their clearance. Then he slipped from their scan and that was it. Nothing. Not another sight of *Interstellar Two Nine*."

"They were actually in orbit around Croton?"

"Yes. It's all on the tape with the record of signals from *Two Nine*."

Fletcher stood up and went back to his window. Vanessa swiveled in her chair to stay facing his way. He was giving lateral thinking a run at the data and its first product seemed way-out.

"Why was the charter arrangement made with us? Southern Hemisphere Space would have been handier."

"Perhaps we were cheaper. They'd be on a budget. Or perhaps there was a waiting period for a suitable ship."

"There wouldn't be any urgency. Customs don't change overnight. Also an organization like that plans a long way ahead."

"Nobody inquired. This is a business organization and we were glad to arrange the charter."

"I'll talk to them. Get me the local director in Brazilia. But before you go, tell me what you have against Bromius."

Vanessa answered from the hatch, "Nothing personal, controller. Just a feeling. They're too good to

10

be true. Nobody can be like that all the time, twenty-four hours a day. It just isn't human."

As he waited for the call, he had to admit that she had a point. They were a living reproach to every thrusting commercial nation. But why be cynical? That was the way it was. Hulda had finally gone, because she had settled for the line of duty rather than personal happiness. Or so it had appeared, without any direct statement.

The video bleeped and then glowed with the orchid pattern of Brazilia's WAIT signal. Fletcher settled in front of it and switched himself in.

The pattern dissolved into a pale green mist which cleared slowly to reveal the head and shoulders of a round-faced type with lips set in a PR grin and kohl-rimmed eyes black as disks of obsidian.

"I am the director's personal secretary. What can I do for you, controller?"

"You can get me the director."

"Dr. Izod is away in your missing ship."

"I know that. There is a local director for the Brazilian sector."

"That is Dr. Cordoban. She is not available."

"When will she be available?"

"Not for some time. She is preparing a small expedition and will be away for several weeks."

Fletcher suddenly had the impression that he was listening to a stall. For some reason Dr. Cordoban did not want to talk to him. He said, "When does she leave on this trip?"

"Early in the morning. There is a great deal to arrange before she leaves. Can I help you?"

"It doesn't matter. Just one thing though. Why did your organization use a European Space charter?"

"Economics, controller. You are very efficient.

11

Your prices were twenty percent cheaper. A foundation like ours has to watch costs."

Fletcher saw the screen blank out and came to a decision. He called Vanessa on the intercom. "Book me on the midday transcontinental for Brazilia. Alert Fairclough that I'll be away for the next twenty-four hours."

"And the chairman?"

"You can tell him when I've gone."

"Will do."

She was not clear what he hoped to gain by it; but it was enough that he was back in action. She even whistled the opening bars of a current hit as she made the connection.

Heavily decorated with squat forms in bas relief, the headquarters of the Institute of Ethnology occupied its own tower block on the north side of a spacious square. Angular abstract shapes dotted with climbing children filled the garden area like a forest. The heat was out of the day. Red dust was raised in small spirals by a buoyant wind blowing over the plateau.

Dag Fletcher moved himself through two reduction bays from the primary lane of the walkway and walked up a broad ramp to the porch.

Seen close, the building was oppressive. Maybe there was something in the flat-headed decoration at that. It could symbolize the human spirit deformed by pressure. One thing was for sure: it housed no tight-wad organization. No expense had been spared in housing the many departments of the Ethnology H.Q.

The lobby had a rich mosaic floor and its walls were paneled with polished yellow wood. In the center, the information kiosk followed the outline of a human heart with the left ventricle all set up to do business as a request station.

He spoke into the orifice, "Where do I find **Dr. Cordoban?**"

There was no hesitation. The robot clerk had not been told she was too busy to see her public. "Floor thirty-one, Room 18A. Please file a request for an interview."

Fletcher was already crossing the parquet. With heavy ethnological humor the elevator offered a choice of cages as if to receive the corpse of the searcher. There was a sarcophagus, an urn or a plushy twentieth-century casket. He chose the first and entered into the spirit of it by crossing his arms on his chest.

Room 18A was facing the outlet across a wide square landing.

Her name was on the door: DR. XENIA CORDOBAN DEPUTY DIRECTOR. He slid it clear and went in to find himself face to face with an old friend.

It was the personal secretary and she looked less than pleased to see him. Her mouth dropped open; her eyes, already large, widened to their physical limit.

He said evenly, "Hello again. I'll see the good doctor. Before she goes on that trip."

If he had come from the sarcophagus trailing a bandage and asking for Isis, she could not have moved faster. One minute she was there and the next she had whipped away into the woodwork, leaving a girl-shaped void and the impression of dancer's thighs flashing briefly below a crotch-length apricot tabard.

Fletcher pushed through a hanging screen of amber amulets and watched the messenger deliver the last phase of a well-told tale.

She was leaned forward in a taut pose over a broad executive desk and appeared to have eyes in the back of her head. But closer study proved it to be an illusion. Dr. Cordoban was looking over her shoulder, and although she was keeping her cool she did not look pleased to see him either.

The deputy director was a long-nosed, classical job with a pale skin unravaged by the sun and wind of field exploration, wearing a deep, elaborate necklace of *lapis lazuli* like a chest protector. Her voice was low-pitched and used English as if it were a thick cream to be spooned out.

"It is usual for visitors to make an appointment."

Her hand was sliding without haste for a bank of studs on the desktop, but Fletcher moved with deceptive speed and intercepted it. At the same time he patted the secretary on her rounded can. "Just run along and listen at the door. I've come a long way for five minutes of the director's time."

An obedient girl, she was halfway to the door before she realized that she had other loyalties. But following Confucian principles, her superior was bowing to the inevitable. She got a small nod and continued through the curtain.

Fletcher said, "Thank you. I shan't keep you long. You know that the charter ship has disappeared. I want to cover every possible angle."

"How can I help you? Surely it is a technical matter?"

"Have you no opinion?"

"Why should I have? From our point of view it is a great loss, of course. Dr. Izod was the greatest expert in his field. But our work is not without risk. We accept that."

"What was the work?"

"Our party was to examine a subculture on Croton. There was—is, in fact—a theory that in spite of present social organization these people are purer types, ethnologically speaking, than the dominant group on that planet. It is likely that they came from some other planet in that system but failed to impose their culture on the indigenous people and slipped back into barbarism."

"So?"

"This has not happened often. Usually it is the other way around and the newcomers set the pace. The theory goes on to suspect that they came from Bromius. Dr. Izod was proposing to do deep hypnotic analysis of a sample group on both planets to try to equate race memories. He believed it was a likely thing."

It was fair enough. There was nothing to hide. His hunch was not paying off.

"What personnel did you send?"

There was a slight hesitation and suspicion came back strength nine. But the reply was ready enough.

"Six from here. Dr. Izod's assistant Juan Gonzales, three other men and two women. They were to pick up Dr. Izod and two others in Fingalna before going on. Nine in all."

"All institute staff?"

Again there was a hesitation. "Work of this kind demands close liaison with many departments. Other experts are sometimes included."

"And were included in this case?"

"I believe Dr. Izod engaged two helpers with special knowledge of the people."

"In Fingalna?"

"That is so."

"Well, thank you. As you say there is nothing that throws a new light on the matter."

"How could there be? You have come a long way

15

to hear what must have been on the charter manifest. What did you expect me to say?"

"I never expect anything. But now I know more than I did. The journey hasn't been wasted."

Eyes in the calm mask were wary. She was going over what she had said and wondering what he was on about.

The voice, however, was at its creamiest. "I am so glad, of course. You must come again when you have more time."

In the lobby below Fletcher was almost through to the porch when he noticed a door marked TRANS-PORTATION and went in without checking his stride. A small bald man with a green eyeshield stopped punching figures onto a feedtape and asked politely, "What is it, Mac?"

"Just a time query. When does Dr. Cordoban leave in the morning on her small expedition?"

"That's easy. She doesn't. That's the first I heard of it and I reckon we'd have to know here to lay on porterage. You've got it wrong, Mac. What's your interest?"

"Actualities coverage. Just a rumor we picked up. But if there's nothing to it we'll have to wait."

It was twenty-three hundred hours on the nose when he let himself into his office. For half its height the headquarters building was a filigree of light but his own sector was isolated, above and below in total blackout.

He called down to the all-night kitchen for coffee and paced around the office until a glow from the service elevator marked its arrival. He lifted out a tray with ceramic ware and a tall silver dispenser and poured himself a cup.

The silence and isolation suited his mood. He took out a cigarette, flipped Neil Walker's first tape of the mission into the actualizer slot, dimmed the lights and took his coffee to the window. Outside the distant ships were floodlit. Inside, the command cabin of *Two Nine* came up bright and clear in the corner of the room.

He was there, present as on many a past mission. He could feel a familiar tightening of the nerves as though he himself would be the one to shove over the red lever that severed the ship's connection with Earth and moved it out into the unknown.

Two Nine was one of the smallest deep-space craft and its control room was barely four meters square. All eight of the crew were crowded in. He knew every one. It was impossible to accept that they were dead and that he had called up their ghosts.

Walker's brisk authoritative voice began the routine outline of the mission. Fletcher listened while he looked around the group. Pete Barry, the copilot, listened with head bowed, hands relaxed in front of him on the console: dark, stocky, very steady. Next to him was Brian Jones, power executive, senior in service on the ship and therefore ranking third, another first-class spaceman. Then John Orchard, navigation executive, long narrow face, fair, one of the best navigators in the service.

Roy Walsh, power no. 2 and Paul Scanton, his opposite number in communications, faced in from the ends of the chart spread. Both were angular, spiky youngsters similar in lifestyle. Scanton wore a short, well-trimmed beard.

Backs to him, the two women crew members had close, functional hair. Delia Loyden was already in a ribbed silver-gray inner suit which outlined shoulders and arms in a smooth flattering sheath. Gerda Triggs, beside her, still wore a square-shouldered tomato-red tabard.

It was as sound a crew as could be hand-picked from the service. Whatever had gone wrong must have been totally unexpected. It was a minimum crew though. Carrying nine of the charter party had meant saving weight on the operational side.

Walker had got to his peroration. Nothing fresh. Just an outline of what he already knew. Clearly the commander of *Two Nine* was not worried by the reduced crew. He ended with, "So. There's a period of one month on Croton, while the research people do their thing. Then the route in reverse with a stop at Fingalna to refuel. Roundtrip under three months. Any questions?"

Fletcher stopped it there and switched to the final tape. Again he got the control room of *Two Nine*. Neil Walker was circling slowly on the command island. Sealed up in full spacegear, identified by the legend COMMAND—I stenciled in Times Bold across his helmet.

The bulky anonymous figure at the power desk with POWER—1 across his shoulders would be Brian Jones. They were following correct procedure for a ship entering orbital path. That in itself showed where they were. The transmission was timed at fourteen hundred hours on day twenty-nine of the mission. They were smack on schedule.

Walker spoke to Croton. The distant voice of the Croton operator using a language filter came over faintly. The transmission ended. Walker stopped his slow circuit. The scene folded in and blanked. He was looking at the plain walls of his office. That was it. There was nothing else.

Fletcher found that his coffee had gone cold. He

went through to the washroom and poured it away, refilled the cup, stubbed the button for a replay and listened again.

On the fourth run through he was with Walker and Jones in that cabin. Tiny aural clues had built up. He had the feel of the ship around him. From countless hours in craft like *Two Nine*, he could fill out the gaps. He found himself swiveling in his chair, answering with Walker as the tape created the scene again and again.

There was something knocking for recognition in the back of his mind and he got to it at the seventh replay. Walker had closed the link early. There was no need to shut down on Croton. In fact, he now believed that he would have held the link open for the rest of the way in.

On the tenth run he was sure of it. He concentrated on the last section of the record, running it again and again.

A small scuff and a click had him spinning his chair to face his own door.

His glare of concentration was so savage that Vanessa was within a narrow point of dropping the tray she was bringing in. She said defensively, "I thought you'd be working through and I brought you some supper."

"Go out and do that again."

It was no greeting for a girl in a hand-embroidered shift with a navel window and a fine electrum chain with a locket, who had cut short a heavy date in the line of duty. But she hooked a supple toe around the hatch and shut herself out.

She tried again. "I thought you'd be working through and I brought you some supper."

She had never rated it as a stupendous speech and it sounded flatter the second time. Fletcher ignored it anyway. He was listening to yet another repeat of the endgame in the command cabin of *Two Nine*.

Now he had it clear. A small sound that had escaped identification was crystal clear. The hatch behind Walker, not in vision, had been opened. That had prompted him to close the link with Croton.

One thing was sure. It was not a change of watch and no other crewman would reappear in an off-duty period. They had seen more than enough of it. That left one of the passengers. What did that mean? An irregularity for a start—but not necessarily serious. After a month in a small ship, crew and passengers would be on close terms.

Swiveling thoughtfully, he saw Vanessa with her tray. "What is it then?"

"I thought you'd be working through and I brought you some supper."

She got immediate proof that even the most banal line repeated often enough takes on cosmic significance. It went like a bomb. He was out of his seat full of zip and brio, and she had a momentary notion that a heavy tray might well be a girl's best friend.

But Fletcher stopped dead at arm's length and said mildly, "Good, good. A very civil gesture. Put it on any convenient flat surface and do something for me. I want to see pictures of the research faction. Get on to Fingalna, the Institute of Ethnology in Argentus. They'll transmit copies of the three who joined the ship there. The six from this end, we should have."

It was an our before she had a full set. Fletcher dimmed the lights and projected them in a line, life-size on his long wall. They fell into three groups and he shuffled the pictures around so that the group characteristics were more marked.

He had gotten himself three academics: Izod small, dark, thin-faced; Dr. Gonzales, graying, smooth-faced, an aging playboy; Dr. Lovenz, late twenties with an adman's flash of choppers.

The three women were in the center: Sorcha Menaldi and Vanora del Rio, medical doctors both—the hypnotists no doubt: small, plump, mid-forties. Reina Vair, listed as Izod's secretary, was out of place. The manifest said she weighed five thousand and ninety grams on the hoof and every last one was asking for attention in white minimal shorts and a crisp candy-striped shirt with buttoned cuffs to boost the stenographer image. Lithe as any panther, if she had been Walker's visitor it would be a powerful counterattraction to the Croton operator.

But it was the trio bunched at the end of the line that had him reaching for a long-distance call. Sangloss, Ross and Guilder would have been way-out in any research setup. He recognized the type. They were hatchet men: heavily built, deadpan, stony-eyed, they had the look of professional killers.

It took some time to raise Xenia Cordoban. When he got her, she was holding a froth of rose madder lace across a chest that was heaving prettily with emotion and her hair was in a tangle not consistent with quiet sleep. She fairly spat out, "This is persecution, controller. What can you possibly want at this time that can't wait until morning?"

It was an opening for wit, but Fletcher asked his own question in a hard and totally uncooperative voice. "What function had Ross and Guilder on your expedition?"

She took a deep breath and it was touch and go whether the lace screen wold keep station. "That is not your business."

"The loss of *Interstellar Two Nine* is my business.

21

It will be I.G.O. business after today, when our report is made. I can be over there with a subpeona in two hours. You could be here 'on call for some weeks as a material witness."

The eyes told him that she hated his guts, but with an effort that nearly strangled her she got her voice to a fair copy of its normal clotted-cream texture.

"There was valuable equipment. Dr. Gonzales wanted protection for the team."

"And Sangloss?"

"The same. Dr. Izod engaged him in Fingalna. Our work takes us amongst very primitive people. It is not unusual to take guards along."

"It is unusual not to declare it on a charter manifest. Commander Walker was not aware of it."

He had taken that shot in the dark. The Brazilian was however already believing that he had the full score.

"There could have been delays. There was a date line. We could not afford to be hung up."

"So you came to us. Southern Space might have recognized your guards. What was the date line?"

"What difference does it make now?"

"What was the date line?"

"If it helps you, May 29th Earth Reckoning. We wanted to begin our inquiries on that date."

Somewhere in the back of his mind there was recognition. He had heard that date mentioned in another context, but he pushed on.

"Why?"

"That would require a great deal of explanation."

"Try me."

"Briefly it has to do with the pattern of race memories. We believed it had to do with important tribal ceremonies. Although their present time scale has changed in a new environment, there could be residual traces."

"That's fair enough. Was there any opposition to your project from Croton or Bromius?"

"The exact details were not known to either. Only Dr. Izod, Dr. Gonzales and myself knew the precise terms of the inquiry."

"You were taking a chance if the findings turned up something they didn't want to know about."

"That is a risk a scientist must be prepared to take. We are concerned with facts and the truth."

"Truth is a big word. Sometimes a dangerous one. Well, thank you. Don't go too far away, you could be needed. *Buenas noches.*"

Vanessa watched the screen fade and said, "Ethnological slut."

"You don't like her?"

"I wouldn't trust her with a big diamond."

Fletcher said, "That wraps it up for tonight. I don't believe there'll be much else from this end. I can recommend to Spencer that we send a search craft to follow the same course. Get some sleep and first thing when you come in let me have a personnel list of all space crew on standby. And thank you. You've been a big help."

It was not until he was parking his personal shuttle in the roof hangar of his apartment block that two matters clarified definitively in his head.

One was that he would command the search craft himself. He needed action to exorcise his loving ghost.

The other was that Hulda herself had spoken of May 29th; but in what connection he could not now remember.

II

Fletcher's name was a draw. Coupled with the rumor that he was taking out the corvette, it was a magnet to bring young men from leave and old men from the brink of retirement. By ten hundred hours the crew manifest could have been filled out twice over with volunteers.

He could understand their point of view. Every serving deep-space crewman had known the frustration of working a schedule in craft that sacrificed power for freight and had to depend on every sophisticated trick in the book to make a planetfall. Also they had known what it was to keep an uneasy security among an alien population, depending on a paper writ and the ultimate power of an I.G.O. task force to take retribution.

But the corvette, *Interstellar X*, was an erstwhile unit of the military force itself. It was powered to handle in an atmosphere like an intercontinental shuttle, its navigational aids were ahead of anything that could be carried on a freight-and-exploration ship of the company and, beyond all, it was still armed.

Even though it was an obsolescent marque it could devastate an area the size of Scotland by a single blast from its main armament.

Bringing the corvette into the company's strength had been a triumph of negotiation on Fletcher's part. His personal influence with I.G.O. military command had finally swung it. The company had been allowed to purchase it at a nominal price with stringent safeguards written into the contract. It was held as a breakdown tender, to pull a crew out of an untenable spot if there were no patrol squadron in the area.

Spencer authorized the request for its use and lumbered into his chief controller's office half an hour before his board meeting with the draft of the I.G.O. clearance.

He found Fletcher making a final selection of crewmen for the manifest and began on an economic gripe.

"Have you any idea what this is going to cost in fuel and man hours?"

"Can we afford not to do it? There's the company's reputation for safe travel to think about. We have to know the answer."

Spencer shifted his ground. "I'm glad you're thinking about that one at long last. I was nicely fixed yesterday I can tell you, with nothing to say except a plea for more time. Made me look stupid."

Fletcher could have said that some had a head-start in that field, but he suppressed it and said, "I'll have a crew by midday. Blast off at eighteen hundred."

"Well, here's the writ. One thing, it may justify having that moldering military scrap on the books. They waive their right to put a serving I.G.O. officer on board as an observer, since you're taking the command. But they insist on a temporary secondment for the duration of the mission. You revert to I.G.O. discipline and control at your honorary rank. I agreed to it. But don't have illusions of grandeur. *Interstellar X* is a civilian ship and you have a civilian crew. No power politics to louse up our trading posts."

"I understand that."

"Have you anything worked out?"

"Not beyond duplicating the flight plan for *Two*

Nine. I'll make a few inquiries in Fingalna and then get to the last reference logged by Neil Walker. See how it looks from there."

"Well, I'd better talk to these zombies. They'll ask why we didn't move before, but I guess I can out-flank that one."

At the door he stopped with his hand on the latch. "Take care of yourself, you represent a lot of invest-ment in training."

"I'll do that. I have the shareholders' interests at heart."

Spencer still took his time to cross the threshold and Fletcher suddenly realized that he had intended to say something else, but was doubtful about it.

That was unusual enough. The chairman was not one for holding back.

When it came it was unexpected. Spencer slewed around from the door and said, "Now that you're back to normal I can tell you. You had me worried. Not like you at all. That Bromusian commissar had you mesmerized. Believe me, Dag, I've seen it happen before. It never works. An alien is an alien is an alien. I'm not blaming you, but I reckon you'll come round to the view that you're well out of it. Good luck."

He was out through the hatch like a bulky jack-rabbit.

Fletcher recognized the sincerity behind it and re-sisted a first impulse to sound off at the closing door.

It reminded him that Hulda had been out of his head for some hours. He could not remember ex-actly what she looked like. There was a residual im-pression of openness and warmth and skin hyaline as alabaster.

Before he could get stuck on a loop, he closed his mind to recall and began to flip over the profile cards of the available deep-space personnel. There was not much to choose between them and he settled for a balanced crew age- and sex-wise, with first regard for the replacement needs of the service ships which would be coming in.

But when he was sealed up on the command island of the corvette with wreaths of white steam clouding the observation ports as the preheating gear drove condensed moisture out of the tubes, he reckoned he was a lucky man. The feel of it was right. He had gotten himself a first-class crew.

In spite of the tumult building on the pad as the motors escalated, they were in a silent world of instrumentation. Five of his eight crew were visible as he revolved slowly on the command island. Cocooned in spacegear and strapped in shock cradles, he checked them off as their responses were cleared by the copilot.

"Power. All systems Go." Frank Holdbrook's deep bass brought its picture of the dark, burly power executive.

"Navigation. All systems Go." Soprano. Elegant and precise. Averil Marr. A promotion for her to be put in as navigation executive.

"Communications. All systems Go." A first time as senior communications for Randle Hobbs.

Then the copilot Jim Scullion at his left, circling with him on the island: "All desks clear, commander."

Fletcher glanced along his console. He had clearance from the unseen emergency centers manned for the countdown sequence. He could visualize them watching their monitors. Sinclair and Wilson, sitting over the power module, would know that any miscalculation would get to them first. The redhead Tamar Kelly, who had proved to be even more spectacular than her color photograph, would be in the tiny compartment below the cone on the subsidiary communications console.

Last man, Diggory Taft, the navigation number two, was in the modified gunnery control with power under his thumb to turn the whole complex into molecular trash. He was recently back in service after a stint with I.G.O. and could double as gunnery officer if it ever came to that.

Fletcher said, "Stand by," and shoved over the red lever that cut them off from all human aid on Earth.

Then she was moving, with an intense flower of flame uncurling like a specimen in time-lapse and thundering along the blast ducts. Gathering urge. Flinging herself into a new dimension.

It was all beginning again as it had so often in the past. They all felt it. This was what bound them to their trade. It was like rebirth. They were moving into a fluid situation where the unexpected was the norm and where anything was possible for the human spirit.

"Day Eight, rationalized time, sidereal plot as charted." Dag Fletcher paused in his log record to give the scanner time to digest the detail on the chart.

So far there was only satisfaction with the mission. Organization under Jim Scullion was moving like refined clockwork. The crew had shaken down into a team. So far there was no awkward member to break the peace. It only needed one in the confined quarters of a spacer to turn the mission into a chore.

Tamar Kelly, communications two, sharing the watch with Sinclair at the power desk, left her console and her tawny mane crossed his line of vision as she navigated around the island.

Neat and compact with a pale freckled skin, very straight nose and a short upper lip, she had more than her ration of restless vitality. Currently she was using it to put a necklock on the seated man at the power desk which seemed likely to lift off his head.

Fletcher released the recording stud and set himself to sort it out.

"Kelly?"

"Here, present, commander."

"What is it, then?"

"He's snatched my lucky dog."

"Sinclair?"

There was no answer. He was short of air.

Fletcher went on: "Give that girl that obscene dog and for the love of God, leave it alone."

When she was back at her desk with the black articulated puppet that took up any one of a thousand grotesque positions each more hideous than the last, he was able to get on. It was something that this childish ritual game the two played was still fairly funny, even to a spectator. He wondered briefly how far the situation developed when they were off-duty. The dog had a lecherous leer at that. Love me, love my dog. Or the other way.

He went on to tell the log that they were approaching the gravisphere of Fingalna, dead on schedule. In six hours he could warp out of rationalized time and prepare for a planetfall at Argentus.

He handed over navigation to Averil Marr with the silver-green planet plate-sized on the main scanner and Argentus control giving a preliminary rundown on data for a proving orbit.

Phase one was ending in copybook style. He thought about the ongoing action briefly in his cabin before he slept solidly like a sailor for the few hours he had. There was not likely to be any new fact to be picked up in Argentus. But he would take three days. The Fingalnians were shrewd. If there were any curious angle on *Two Nine*'s mission it would not have escaped notice.

Averil Marr conned them in, clearly delighted to handle the ship, in a display of cool timing that exploited all the technical resource of the corvette.

Interstellar X flexed on her hydraulic rams and wreathed herself in a shroud of gray coolant. She was all set for a military-type arrival with a task force spilling out to hold a bridgehead.

Fletcher spun the scanner and looked around the port. They had been given a berth on the inner circle, next to a Fingalnian interceptor craft. There were very few empty pads. Fingalna had climbed back into the big league as a galactic trading post. Memories were short. It was not so long ago that she had been drawn into the gamble of the Outer Galactic Alliance and teamed with the subhuman hatchet men of Scotia and Chrysaor to end the peaceful hegemony of the InterGalactic Alliance.

It was hard to tell whether there had been a real change of heart, but there was no gainsaying they gave the impression of total welcome.

Receding lines of pale green undulating downs marched to the horizon on every side. Argentus was in a shallow bowl, a delicate city of white pinnacles and suspended walkways like silver streamers thrown over an elaborate cake.

The spaceport call-sign glowing on the scanner was a silver seahorse on a cerulean backdrop. Since they had nothing more to say reception-wise, the control tower had switched to faint tinkling music, nearest by Earth standards to a Cambodian temple orchestra, which added a last dimension of fantasy.

They had arrived in Arabian Nights territory where any bottle might hold a jinn.

First call at the European Space office in the Earth Consulate block was negative. Polyxo, the Fingalnian manager of the terminal, was anxious to oblige but had nothing to tell. Small and silvery-skinned with the seemingly ageless bland face of his race, he sat at his desk, with his hands clasped in front of him, scratching the back of his left wrist with a long delicate thumb. His voice was soft and sibilant.

"I met Commander Walker of course. The arrangements to pick up Dr. Izod were made here. We checked weight and equipment against the manifest. I have it here. There was not much. Only hand baggage. All their stores had been loaded by the main party at your end."

Polyxo had the document ready and handed it over. He was right. There was nothing to it. Reina Vair looked all set for any lechery, but there was nothing sinister in that. Sangloss was a natural for a wanted poster, but was apparently armed only with a nailfile and a gold-plated toothpick.

"What did you think of Dr. Izod?"

"I saw him several times. He booked in at the terminal two days before *Two Nine* arrived. He seemed anxious to get away. He was always very courteous and pleasant, but he inquired every few hours about time schedules. He wanted a duplicate of the flight plan to Croton. That is unusual."

"But you gave him one?"

"Of course, controller. The customer may be wrong, nevertheless he is always right—as I believe you say on Earth planet."

"What did you make of Sangloss?"

Polyxo scratched thoughtfully as though reluctant

to speak ill of the dead. "I did not care for him. Many nationalities come to Fingalna. There is much riffraff. After the war there was money to be made in many doubtful enterprises. I am sorry to say it, but you can still hire men and women in Argentus who would do anything you ask for a fee. He seemed to me to be one of those. He and the woman did not go naturally with Dr. Izod."

Polyxo changed his grip and scratched gently at his other wrist. Fletcher waited patiently. There was something else to be said and he knew from experience that Fingalnians should not be rushed.

Outside, the pale green pallor of the sky was deepening to the viridian dusk of Fingalna. Lights in the terminal were automatically adjusting to keep the lumen count steady at the optimum level for eye comfort.

"I had the impression, controller, that Sangloss and Miss Vair were working together against the doctor and that in some way he was following their instructions. That is a very personal judgment and I have nothing definite to base it on."

"That's interesting. But it doesn't take us far into the loss of the ship. It was lost with all hands. Sangloss doesn't look the type to sacrifice himself for a cause."

"I agree, controller. I have asked myself many times what could possibly have happened out there and each time I can find no reasonable answer."

"Where did Sangloss come from?"

"This is the address he gave. It is in the downtown area. Not a good neighborhood. He had a room there. I hope you will not think of going there alone."

First there was his crew to think about. With Scullion, he worked out a relief plan to keep the

32

ship at standby readiness and give all personnel a stint at the bright lights. When it was done and the corvette's small patrol car was hovering at the main hatch, he joined the first shore party.

Dave Sinclair, Tamar Kelly, Averil Marr and Diggory Taft had drawn the lucky numbers and were bound for the casino that dominated the central square in the pleasure quarter.

The navigation executive, who had been there before, was in the pilot slot, wearing the green-and-gold ceremonial tabard of the line; short, intensely black hair was dramatized by an electrum headband studded with brilliants. Beside her, Tamar Kelly had opted for a black chain-link shift barely crotch-length, with her flamboyant red-gold hair swinging like an elastic bell.

Fingalnian courtesy took a knock when the small car sidled into a docking collar on the vast parking lot on the open roof.

Malvina's, the most spectacular building in a fantastic city, was an inverted pyramid, balanced at its tip on a meter-diameter stud and transparent through its length and depth. It was already thronged with people who appeared to be filling its volume like space walkers distorted into moving segments of brilliant color by a thousand filters of curved glass.

The small Fingalnian commissionaire who hurried forward with a set grin of welcome, stopped in his tracks and his jaw dropped. He watched Tamar Kelly move with supple grace through the hatch and stood rooted to the deck.

Her lucky dog, hanging over her arm with its paws limp with sin, had fixed him with its glittering eye and he was still motionless when Fletcher, last through the hatch, joined the tail end of the party.

Reassured by the uniform, he said, "I have seen some strange sights in this place, but never anything like that. What kind of animal is that, please?"

"It's a dog. You see them all the time on Earth."

"Then it is not surprising, if you will excuse me, that so many Earthmen are travelers. You would wish not to see them I think."

"It's her mascot. It brings good luck."

"Not to anyone who has to look at it, I think. It makes me go sick to my stomach. Welcome anyway. I hope you will enjoy yourselves."

Music sighed through the intricate complex of transparent rooms, drifting up and down on a scheme of rhythm and melody that was outside reason. Color and perfume, infinitely subtle, drifted through every permutation open to the five wits; Fingalnian voices tinkled like small silver bells. It was the house of unknowing. Circe's house.

Only Tamar Kelly's depraved dog struck a discordant note. He was outside the range of any charm. When she stood him beside her elbow at a table, a nervous croupier dropped his rake and an elderly Mandarin type, who had been drinking the local Melissean wine from a triangular beaker, leaned forward, shook a bony finger at it and slowly toppled forward until his forehead was resting on the green cloth.

Tamar Kelly threw a blue chip on a starfish symbol and waited for action. Drawn by a kind of reluctant fascination, people left nearby tables and made a tight circle. It was going to be an unusual night.

Fletcher allowed himself to be edged into the outer ring. It was like pushing through a collection of human-sized butterflies. Most of the Fingalnian women followed the traditional style of their culture;

34

delicately modeled, silvery-skinned, they carried the bulk of their clothing in elaborately wired trains behind them, leaving frontal treatment exclusively to narrow harness straps of gold and electrum and jeweled clips wherever forward-planning nature had supplied a holdfast.

He stopped apologizing partly because few could understand and partly because nobody was listening. They were all watching Tamar and her dog. He would not be missed.

At a long verandah, he called an auto shuttle from a console and it dipped out of a line that was circling the middle floor to pick him up. In the small cab, he fished out the address that Polyxo had given him and dialed it into the robot pilot.

The shuttle rose into an interzonal connector, waited in the queue for a place, and joined the main stream. Argentus was a kaleidoscope of color and light, totally different from its day image of white sugar icing. A human pilot would have been totally baffled. There seemed to be no sense or pattern in it. But the auto shuttle locked on to its selected beam path and weaved through the confusion, choosing its time to drop like a stone into lower flight paths, spinning on its axis in ninety degree turns until he was out of the metropolitan area.

Traffic thinned. The shuttle was passing only a few meters above the highest walkways. Even the flattering street lighting could not conceal an air of gimcrack in the tall apartment buildings on either side. There were very few citizens up and about and those were in groups.

A patrol car came up from behind, hovered alongside while its four man crew stared into the shuttle and then pulled ahead.

For a moment, he expected it would stop and use its special switchgear to ground him, but it picked up speed and turned off at the next intersection.

The red indicator line on the town plan was almost at the reference he had dialed. The shuttle slowed, distanced itself midway between two walkways and dropped sixty meters in freefall. Then it sidestepped to a monorail, hooked on, and ran under the cover of a long bare porch, dimly lit from ceiling ports.

Fletcher checked the address with his paper. Ophion House. He was home and dry.

A succession of glass doors sealed off the entrance. He could see into a reception area with plain numbered doors opening off it and a central kiosk with two elevator trunks.

Getting in was another matter. Residents would have passkeys. There was no open door, and when he pressed the summoning stud for the janitor there was no movement from the empty lobby.

At the third attempt the extreme left-hand inner door suddenly changed to a bright oblong and an old Fingalnian in a brown belted smock shuffled out into the hall. He crossed as far as the kiosk and leaned on it for a spell, clearly doubting the wisdom of opening up.

Fletcher waved his piece of paper, pointed to it and crossed both hands on his chest. It was the local sign for peace and goodwill, but coming from a two-meter tall alien in a poor light it was only a small collateral for security.

Curiosity carried the day. The ancient Fingalnian hobbled forward and opened a slot in·the glass. It was level with Fletcher's sternum and he had to stoop to talk through it. He would have liked to say, "Harry said knock twice and ask for Rachel," but he reckoned it would lose its nuance in speech tones. So he used the Galactic *lingua franca* in the traditional greeting: "Peace on this house."

Surprised, but going along with a trier, the oldster wheezed out the standard answer:

"And to the stranger."

"I want to talk to the janitor about a man who lived here."

"That is not possible. As you see the desk is closed for the night. I act on his behalf when he is not here. Who are you?"

"Do you recognize this uniform? I am an officer in the I.G.O. peace force."

"At night a cotton seed is the same as a pearl."

There was a ring of truth in that one and some other touchstone was called for. "I will pay for information. Here are fifty creusas."

Fletcher opened out a bill and passed it through the slot.

"What do you want to know?"

"I would like to see the room where the man lived. He was called Sangloss. This is his picture."

The man flattened his small nose to the glass and peered short-sightedly at exhibit A. Recognition seemed to encourage trust. It was all true; the stranger was right. "Yes. There was such a man. I remember him. I did not like him."

"I don't like him either."

It was agreement. Coupled with this friendly habit of posting currency through the door, it put Fletcher in a new light as an ally in the life situation.

"Wait."

He hobbled back to the kiosk, lifted a flap and disappeared inside. Seconds later, the glass section in front of Fletcher slid aside. As he stepped through, it closed smartly at his back. If there were any move they would have to pay their way.

His guide reappeared. "Come. I will show you. But you must be quick. I would not like it to be known that I allowed you to do this. He lived on this floor. Room nineteen. This way."

They passed his own door which was still open and Fletcher saw a bare room with one chair, a low table and a divan bed. In the corner, a small actualizer was still showing a program on a meter-cube set: one of the traditional, everlasting plays that were incomprehensible to any but the Fingalnians, with no discoverable plot and an endless succession of costume characters.

Age in any culture amounted to the same thing. It was a waiting time and a shadow play was as good as anything else to fill it.

A narrow corridor with doors either side led off to the left. Number nineteen was the last room. Beyond it was a spiral stair for the athletically minded and a street exit closed for the night. Close to the door, it was ideal for a man who might want visitors or who might want to move in and out without too much notice.

In this last, however, Sangloss had reckoned without the interest of the old man.

"I sleep very little. I sit in my room and think about my past life. I did not expect to end my days in such a place. This man Sangloss was often out at night. He stayed here for about thirty days. His room has not been let because he paid a quarter in advance."

"Who were his visitors?"

"Earthmen like yourself. A woman, who stayed with him for several days. And just before he left there was one I heard but I did not see. That one I did not like at all. I was in the Fingalnian fleet at the time of the troubles and they were our allies, but I never liked them. They are not human as we are human and you Earthmen are human."

"How could you tell who it was if you did not see him?"

"The language was plain. He was using a scrambler to turn his sounds into speech tones. It was a Scotian."

That left no area for doubt. The atonal system of palatal clicks that passed for a communications system on the bleak planet of Scotia was unique and unmistakable. Once heard it was not forgotten. Even a simple request for the time of day sounded like a rattlesnake winding up for a strike.

At the door of room nineteen, the old man looked both ways, found that they were the only protagonists on the set and pulled a thin metal strip out of a pouch in his belt. He fished delicately in the lock and they were in.

The Fingalnian closed the door and stood with his back to it. "You must be quick. I would not like it known that I allowed this."

There was not much to see. Sangloss traveled light. There was an unmade bed with a brown traveling rug on it; a dressing chest with a crumpled cigarette pack; a small closet with the door open and a metal cloth tabard on a hanger. Drawers in the chest were half pulled out as though, at the last, the man had packed in a hurry. On a chair there was a familiar blue-and-white brochure. He had been studying European Space Corporation schedules.

Altogether it was an unlikely hideout for a man who was known to a distinguished ethnologist and chosen by him as a companion on an important mission. There was a video on a bracket in the corner with a locked metering box.

Fletcher said, "How did he pay for outgoing calls?"

"The record is examined every ten days and a bill is made out."

"Does the record show the numbers called?"

"Of course."

"Could I see that?"

"It will be in the kiosk. Wait here. I will look."

When the door closed, Fletcher sat in a chair. For all the good he was doing he might have stayed at his desk on Earth. What did it matter who Sangloss had spoken to? The answer, if there were one, could only be found in the spacelane where *Two Nine* had foundered. He was wasting his time.

At the end of five minutes he was more than ever convinced. Sangloss was a cheap hood. Period. Leave it at that and get on with the angle he knew about.

Coming to a decision, he opened the door and put out the light. There was no sign of Methuselah in the corridor, nor was his door open when he reached the lobby. Maybe he had had enough and had gone back to his actualizer.

The kiosk flap was still hinged away and Fletcher went to look inside. At first it appeared empty; then he saw the old man as a brown shadow in the well. He was face forward, out of program—curiously light and fragile as Fletcher turned him over.

The silvery ichor that served the Fingalnian variant of the human stock as life's blood was welling from a small hole in the center of his forehead.

On the desk a punched card file had been pulled from a nest. Tabs showed room numbers. Fletcher thumbed along to nineteen and saw that the slot was empty.

At the same time a keening wail started up in the street, growing stronger as its source neared Ophion House. In a flash of intuition, he knew how it would be. His visit had been monitored from the start. Some quick thinker had seen the way to make capital out of it. Not only had it been neatly fixed so that he took no useful information with him, but he was landed with a *corpus delicti* to explain away.

Fingalnian justice was notoriously slow. He could spend the next month in a precinct cell before he was allowed to call a lawyer. That was the angle, of course. *Interstellar X* would be grounded indefinitely until harbor dues shoved the whole exercise into a nonsense bracket and the search was called off.

The shadow of a long police shuttle, probably the one that had paced him earlier, swept into the porch.

Fletcher bent double and ran for the corridor. He shoved open Sangloss's door and put the light on. They would be sure to spend a minute looking at that. Then he went up the treads of the spiral stair two at a time.

As far as he could judge, the walkway he had passed in the shuttle as it homed on the ground floor porch hit the building at the sixth or seventh floor.

At the fifth he stopped and knelt down to put his ear to the center post. A faint rhythmic thump told him that somebody in a hurry had started up.

Fingalnian gravity was slightly below Earth-level, but he was carrying more weight than a bird-boned Fingalnian. On a long haul they were sure to outpace him. He zipped down a flap in the waist of his tabard and pulled out a small flat laser. As he moved on, he set it for a wide-angle nonlethal beam, remembering that if he used it there would be no evidence that the missing charge had not found its way into the janitor's head.

At floor six, he listened again. The beat was stronger, irregular, more than one pair of feet. He ran along the corridor and met his first resident. A

41

Fingalnian girl had opened her door and was two paces out. There was an impression of a startled face and a silvery nude back and she was gone like a rabbit. Her door slammed as he reached the central area.

It was arranged as a lounge with long upholstered settles and small tables, a social center for the floor, much stained and delapidated with one meager light burning from a ceiling port. But the street wall was solid to waist height. There was no walkway outlet at that point.

Fletcher went on, banking that the spiral stair would be duplicated at the far end. It was. But a quick check at the sounding post told him that at least one gendarme was on the way up.

He made the next pitch in a record run and peeled off along the corridor. The floor plan was the same, but through the long window of the lobby wall he could see the static walkway meeting a verandah and the center sections made a double-leaf door.

It was locked and he used some seconds resetting his laser for a beam that melted out the wards.

It was not until he was through and running for the spidery static way that he saw the car out of the corner of his eye. The pilot had edged in to the side of the building with the blunt snout of the tender level with the baluster and had the front port open. He had a squat-barreled riot gun cradled against his cheek and cleverly switched on a spotlight without losing aim. At the same time he spoke through a loud hailer: "Stand still. No one is to leave the building."

In a brief flash of analysis Fletcher reckoned he had a choice of two bad options. If he were taken now he would be out of action for God knew how long. If he got around this one, he would have been identified and would be picked up later. There were not many Earth nationals about in I.G.O. uniform.

Instinct made the choice. While he was a free agent, there was a chance he could do something about it.

He stopped dead, turned smartly to face the car as though going along with the deal, and took a snap shot into the glowing eye of the beam.

At the same time, he threw himself sideways towards the open end of the static way.

A number of things happened at once. The light went out with a plosive crack. From being pinpointed in a pool of brilliant light he became a blurred shadow. The riot gun coughed into life and a bright green tracer flared through the space he had just left. The pilot decided it was an all-hands job, cued in his siren and put out a call to report progress to his section leader.

Fletcher covered the hundred meters above the square at a sprint. The walkway forked, curving left and right along the face of the opposite block. Room lights were going on in every building as the residents reacted to the riot call.

Fletcher moved right, skirted the side of the building, found a ramp going down and joined another static way that led between blocks to the next zonal interconnector. Then he let random choice have its head. If anybody were working out a logical plan to anticipate his route he would be doomed to frustration.

Eventually he must strike a metropolitan throughway with all-night moving walkways.

When he did, he had been at a steady jog trot for ten minutes and sweat was running down his chest. It was like coming out of a tunnel into bright day and he stopped at the intersection to weigh it up.

There were enough people on the fast-moving central lane to give some cover. All roads led to Rome. He could get to the central square, join his party at Malvina's and work it out from there.

There was another hundred meters to go along the sidewalk before a reduction bay system allowed him to filter on to the walkway. He took it at a slow walk, as though he had all the time in the world, with heightened sensitivity in the back of his neck expecting an official voice to sound in either ear.

But there was none. On the walkway he stood with a group, all motionless, suspended in time as their bodies were whisked through the city. He could consider where they had come from, where they were going, whether they were kind or cruel to the cat and whether, like himself, they were a pair of eyes looking out from a closed room with no doors for a visitor.

Except one. Except one. Hulda had been inside or he had imagined it.

It was illusion. There were no exits either. She had not been in or she could not have gotten out.

Fletcher told himself that he was emotionally immature. Soft at the center. It was time he came to terms with a basic fact of the human situation. One is one and all alone and ever more shall be so.

The old song filled his head and he was working on ten for the ten commandments when the walkway swept him into the main square of Argentus with Malvina's stupendous pyramid near enough to hit with a rock.

III

Facing Malvina's across the width of the square, a jutting trapezoid made a nice composition for the tourist photographer. The casino standing on its head, the hotel defying gravity: it was clear proof that life among the stars was more bizarre than anything to be had in Clacton or Pittsburgh.

Sitting in their windowseats with a transparent floor panel, the privileged clientele could get a plain view of the set, with the crowd depersonalized into colored ribbons weaving along the merging and separating walkway systems.

This regular flow set up a standing wave which might lead a philosophic mind to speculate on a kind of immortality. Given commuters moving at a steady rate, the overall pattern had a life of its own, irrespective of the transient human elements that made it up.

Immortality for the biological building blocks was another matter. There were too many on the bandwagon to make it feasible, and too few with any clue of what to do with it if they had it coming.

On floor twenty-three, a gray-skinned Crotonian was in fact watching the swirl of biological material, as though overseer of an open plan sewage farm. His face, no handy mirror for emotion, remained unmoved and colorless as he suddenly leaned forward with both hands on the sill.

The unmistakable figure of an Earthman had separated out of the ruck and was working through the reduction bays towards the cable-car connector with the casino.

The Crotonian said, "Surely that is the commander

45

of the Earth ship. Your overcomplicated plan has miscarried, Labrad. The simplest solution is always the most effective. Assassination in this case. I hope there is still time to arrange it."

Labrad, a Bromusian, similar in build and cephalic index to the speaker, but with a pale ivory skin, hurriedly swept a number of ore samples into a compartmented display case and took it with him to the window.

This cautious move was not lost on a third man sitting well out of the direct light of a powerful standard lamp. His elongated blue-white face took on a sardonic twist and leathery lips wreathed away to show a full set of parallel bony ridges and a narrow reptilian tongue.

Although speaking through a transducer which he wore like a Tudor ruff around the collar of his uniform jacket, he got off the mark before the prudent drummer. "It is all one. Leave him to me. He will not get far from Fingalna. Neither he nor his ship. That is the better way. They will not chance the loss of a third."

The two at the window exchanged glances. Labrad's said plainly enough: "You are the senior. You him."

Unzi weighed his words. He was aware that a Scotian was a difficult ally and that a point could easily be reached where long-term advantage was ignored in favor of present satisfaction. "You are a soldier, Tyro, and think like a soldier. But we cannot afford a military showdown at this stage. We should still aim to make them abandon their inquiry because of difficulties. Direct intervention from an I.G.O. squadron must be avoided. My orders are clear on that."

"I understand. But my ship is an unknown factor.

46

I can take off from the asteroid and overtake that ancient scrap heap before they are inside the Croton system. They would be dispersed as gas before they could identify their attacker."

"It may come to that. But it is a risk we should not take unless it is unavoidable."

"Nevertheless, I will return to my ship and prepare to intercept. If this is not required I will be ready to take one or both of you to O.G.A. headquarters with your detailed report of the level of infrangom in the ore samples. They will be pleased to have proof that the deposits are rich enough to justify any action."

Unzi said, "Fletcher has taken the cable car to the casino. He will rejoin his party. But police reports will be building up a picture of his movements. He is sure to be interrogated."

A police car passed almost level with their window, checked, rose to a high flight lane and disappeared over Malvina's roof.

Labrad said, "You may well be right. But we cannot be sure that he will be implicated. I suggest that we set a limit of one complete day on our efforts. After that the ship should be allowed to leave and Tyro will deal with it."

"Very well." The Crotonian watched Fletcher transfer from the car to the open porch and then disappear into the many-hued pyramid. "There may be an opportunity now. I will see what can be done. Perhaps you would entertain the commander a little longer, Labrad. In any event, I will be back within the hour."

There was silence when he had gone. Labrad, more sensitive to atmosphere, shifted uneasily under Tyro's unwinking stare. This one would sour' the milk in a dedicated P.R.O.

After three minutes, examining and rejecting a number of good opening lines, he said, "It was very opportune, commander, that your ship should be in this quarter. Otherwise we would have had difficulty in making quick contact with O.G.A."

"It is not accidental. Ever since the report from the Earthman that there was infrangom on Bromius, we have maintained a squadron on the frontiers of I.G.O. space. One ship in turn has been on standby, either here or in Croton. There is one thing I do not understand and perhaps you can tell me?"

"What is that?"

"Infrangom is important to any planet with a space program. Why did the Earthman offer his information to O.G.A.? Why risk such danger to himself?"

Tyro did not say, "Why betray his own people?" —the concept of selling any product for gain was good enough as a motive; but the idea occurred to the Bromusian. He was even further involved as a speculator in the natural wealth of his own planet.

"It is not easy to explain."

"We have time."

"On the first expedition Dr. Izod made to Bromius, he was accompanied by a Fingalnian who had served with O.G.A. in the great struggle for liberation. This man had kept his wartime contact with O.G.A. intelligence and offered to act as a go-between."

"That does not say why."

"You have to understand that there are other driving forces beside money. Dr. Izod was working in a field where the political barriers of I.G.O.–O.G.A. were inconvenient and cut across the ethnic groups he was studying. He wanted to be the first scientist to produce a comparative study of all the cultures on the Rim. He believed his accidental find of infrangom might give him a lever to secure access to the O.G.A. planets."

"Did he not know that a deal was already being made and that his knowledge was dangerous?"

"We are not fools. Agents were planted in his organization. He was under constant watch."

"What happened to the charter flight then?"

Labrad shifted evasively, followed by the un-blinking reptilian stare of the Scotian. "That was a local decision in Bromius and had nothing to do with the infrangom agreement."

"A convenient coincidence."

"You could say that."

"Although I say it, I do not believe it. Like the presence of my ship. Coincidence is seldom so con-venient."

Tamar Kelly saw Fletcher arrive at the rear of the crowd. His reflected image was given back by a slowly shifting electrum disk revolving on its edge on a black basalt plinth. Farther right and then dead ahead, she saw Fingalnian security guards in Lin-coln green with carbines on slings and gunmetal riot hats. By an act of intuition, which went right to the heart of the exercise, she knew that there was a connection—that she hadn't seen him for the last hour because he had been elsewhere and the posse was looking for him now.

In the circumstances an alibi couldn't be bad.

She picked up her lucky dog as though to shift him to a point where his malevolent magic would have more scope and nudged over an unsteady pile of blue chips.

They ran in a shimmer over the translucent floor and the nearest Fingalnians broke ranks in a helpful scramble to pick them up. The static scene went fluid for a short count and when the circle reformed Fletcher was at her side as though he came with the furniture.

Tamar, throwing a dazzling smile to all and some, pushed the reassembled mound of counters onto the sign of the lotus.

There was a tangible surge in tension and a hiss of indrawn breath as the sporty crowd reacted to a maximum stake going for the longest shot on the table.

There was a delay while the croupier made a check. With the luck she had been having, Tamar was the last one he wanted on that square. Paid a percentage of the night's overall gain for his station, he was seeing her in the light of a sheaththief who was all set to snatch the last crust of black bread from his children's outstretched hands. He looked at his time disk and saw that the automatic closure would come down in three minutes, forcing her to move herself and her diabolical puppet to another table.

Fletcher saw the look and guessed its meaning. He said, "There is time. The chips are down. Play."

Reluctantly the croupier shoved over an elegant green lever and a jeweled replica of the triangular casino shot into the air in random flight, buffeted from left and right by unseen jets and followed by every eye as it made a glittering progress to the far end of the table where each symbol was represented by a 3D model with an open mouth to catch the airborne pyramid.

Those sited in the center were favorite and attracted the smallest gain. Outlying units like the lotus were statistically unlikely to catch the die and carried high odds.

At fifty to one the lotus was least favored on the board.

The pyramid had reached the apogee of its flight path and was dropping to a target. Air jets released by a random selector went into spasm and shunted it every which way. Everybody in the neighborhood was silent watching it home on the pad. It was lined up on a lizard with a gaping mouth and the croupier looked as happy as a man with aching feet could be in the small hours. Then a freak gust slewed it half a meter across the board and it clunked definitively into the open petals of the lotus.

There was a spontaneous clap. Sinclair, who had been treasurer for the enterprise, began to gather the harvest of blue chips that spewed down a mobile chute. The security guards, frozen for the duration of the action, moved on.

As the leader came within earshot, Tamar Kelly said in her clear positive voice: "That's it then. Do you think we should go, commander, leave while we're ahead? Thank you anyway for staying beside me. You on one side and my lucky dog on the other was the combo that beat the system."

Double billing with the dog was no compliment to any living creature. Sinclair behind her chair looked surprised, took a sharp dig in the lower abdomen from the gambler and contributed, "Oh. Ah," to the conversation.

Tamar Kelly went on, "Don't you agree, Dave? We must ask Commander Fletcher to join us again. If he doesn't mind, that is."

Sinclair was not on the e.s.p. net, but he reckoned the tone was demanding the answer yes. So he gave it, with moderate enthusiasm, and was taken up by a Fingalnian security guard who had pushed patiently through the press and was at his elbow, with an open folder of identity photographs.

"Are you saying, Mr. Sinclair, that Commander Fletcher has been with you all night?"

Before he could speak Tamar Kelly was around in a supple twist that sent her hair surging over her head in red-gold shockwaves.

In the prevailing silver and platinum blonde decor, her hair was the most striking single object on the set and the policeman looked at it as though it were an illusion. Using speech tones to make sure there was no communications problem she said, "We have no complaint, officer. The table is fairly run. I am sure Commander Fletcher will agree."

Fletcher felt like a child with adults talking over his head and put in a word on his own account. "What is it? Is there some problem with the ship?"

The policeman looked from one to the other, uncertain how to act. He had received an all-cars radio call that an Earthman in the uniform of an I.G.O. commander had murdered a janitor in a downtown apartment house and was wanted for interrogation. An anonymous call to the precinct security headquarters had said that Commander Fletcher of the ship *Interstellar X* was the man involved and could be found in the casino.

But there had been malicious calls before. It would certainly not help establish his reputation as a suave cosmopolitan operator to arrest the wrong man and have an interplanetary diplomatic row.

He said, "Not your ship, commander. There is a small matter which has come up which you might help to clear. Perhaps you would be good enough to make a statement at the precinct office."

"Now?"

"Now, if you please. It will not take long."

Tamar Kelly had gathered all her chips on a pink tray and called across two tables to where Diggory

Taft and Averil Marr were still treading fortune's wheel. "Digger. Work for you. Cash this lot for me and don't lose it or a virgin's curse will blear your eye. We have to go to the precinct brig with the commander. Take the car and tell Jim lad to leave the door open."

The policeman said uneasily, "It is not necessary. Only the commander is required to make a statement."

There was no more she could do. But it was enough. She had set it up so that Fletcher could say naturally, "It will save time if a countersignature is needed. Also I should like witnesses of my own, in case I have any complaint to make myself."

Tamar Kelly carried her dog by a hind leg and it hung limply like something that had been dead when the galaxy was young. It was as good as a leper's bell and cleared a path through the press. Social chat died the death. It was a reminder that human life was finite and that there were no pockets in a shroud.

Commissioner Veck, top hand in the Argentus security network, was less than pleased to be pulled from his bed by a blue alert, but nothing of it showed in his eyes or in his neat mandarin dress. He could have been sitting behind his executive console from choice on a routine midmorning stint when Fletcher was wheeled in by a security guard.

He had reached the top dead center of the Fingalnian life cycle where aging seemed to stop. His silvery skin was a network of fine wrinkles. He looked too frail to be allowed out and about. He would stay that way without visible change for the next twenty years and then go out like a light.

To Fletcher the scene was a replay of an earlier confrontation which had been by Veck's own devising and he waited for the man to claim a modest advantage.

But Veck said, "Sit down. Sit down, commander. As soon as I was told that you were in difficulties with the law I decided that I should deal with the matter personally. See you myself. As I know from experience, you have an individual approach to your problems. Why did you find it necessary to visit Ophion House?"

The voice was no more than a whisper, conserving vital resources, unemphatic but bell-clear. It seemed churlish to contradict.

Fletcher said, "In the first place you have no right to bring me here. I went along with your precinct fugleman, like any good citizen, to answer a question. He had no brief to bring my party to security headquarters without allowing me to contact the I.G.O. commissar. I do not have to remind you of diplomatic privilege."

"And I do not have to remind you that local law has to be observed. This is a sovereign state. Allow me to judge what I can do and cannot do. I believe there is an understanding between us. You know that I keep my word. You can trust me with the truth in this matter. Now I am quite certain that you would not go out of your way to kill an inoffensive doorkeeper. Why should anyone go to the trouble of making it appear that you did?"

"So that's what I'm supposed to have done? I know your organization, commissioner. If there is any information, you will have it. Perhaps you could tell me?"

Veck sighed. It was going to be one of those nights. He tried open frankness which would have melted a black basalt rock. "I know of course why you are here. We expected there would be an inquiry into the loss of your ship, and who better to conduct it than yourself with your wide experience in this part of the galaxy. I admired your part in the recovery of the *Leviathan*, although the final solution was against Fingalnian interest. I bear no ill will. Believe me, I bear no ill will. I can let you have the results of the inquiries we made ourselves. In return I would like to know what happened tonight at that tenement. I assume that you went there in the first place to check on the man Sangloss."

It would have been very easy to say, "That's right"—and take it from there. But Fletcher remembered the sophisticated circuitry in Veck's office. No doubt every word was going on record. A little editing and Veck would have a confession to be played in court and a cast-iron case for a maximum penalty.

"You go too fast. I am here to inquire into the loss of *Interstellar Two Nine*. And information you can give will be welcome. I.G.O. is interested. As the I.G.O. officer in charge of the investigation I expect to receive all the help you can give. Now I would like to go back to my ship."

Fletcher stood up and took two steps towards the hatch.

Veck's green eyes narrowed with irritation, but his voice was on the same unruffled note as he said, "You are too hasty, commander. Altogether too hasty. I remember well that you have this fault. You should not refuse help so quickly. Sit down again. In a few minutes I will have you returned to your ship."

Dag Fletcher stood behind the chair, both hands on its functional tubular back, and looked down at the small Fingalnian. He said nothing, reckoning that the fewer words of his they had on tape, the more difficult it would be to fix a phony dialogue.

Veck went on: "Dr. Izod is well-known. The assistants he took from here are also well-known, in a different way. It surprised me that he should employ them. I can let you have detailed profiles of Sangloss and the woman Vair. In return I would be glad of any new information you may find. I should warn you, though this will be quite useless, that there may be more to the loss of your ship than appears, and you could be in great danger. My judgment is that the accident was not planned, but the party of ethnologists were involved in something other than what they pretended. You will have to be very careful."

He stood up and pushed a button on his console. The hatch slid away and a guard with a carbine stepped smartly in.

"Commander Fletcher and his companions are to be taken to their ship. They are not implicated in the affair at Ophion House."

On the threshold Fletcher said, "Thank you, commissioner. I appreciate your help. Good night."

Tamar Kelly, ankles crossed, hair in a smooth fan, had gone to sleep on a reclining chair in the reception area, with Dave Sinclair moodily reading a handbook on flower arrangement and the dog standing on three legs with a forepaw lifting one bedraggled ear as though listening for any evil that might be coming that way.

Fletcher leaned over the back of her chair and put a hand flat on either shoulder. The fine metallic mesh was cool to touch. Seen in reverse and for once very still, her face was regular as a carved classical mask and his mind was hooked on a mathematical analysis of it. Her eyes opened, turning a lay figure into a person with human rights of privacy. He was near enough to see that they were very unusual items: very brown with a golden fleck that was not seen

56

from a distance; steady and untroubled, as though waking in a strange prison was natural in any long day.

Sinclair said, "Wake up Kelly. It's time you were in your trundle bed."

Fletcher moved his hands, suddenly conscious they had been there too long. She rolled smoothly out of the sack and gathered up her dog, not looking at either of them.

To underline the fact that they were as free as any bird, Veck had whistled up a commercial shuttle to meet them at the porch. It was a luxury job with alternate sets of dual bucket seats and tables on an observation platform with aisles either side and a human pilot, who spoke up in English to make them feel wanted. "Where do you wish to go, Excellency?"

"The spaceport. Berth 17. The Earth ship *Interstellar X*."

Whether deliberately or not, Sinclair isolated the girl on the double squab behind the pilot and Fletcher was separated from them by the width of a table.

The car pulled away into a lane-change zone and waited for a gap in the busy trans city freeway. Late late shows were closing and there was a minor traffic peak on. Fletcher sat back and tried to weigh progress. There was not a lot. But to be out of the security pen was something. Veck could have played it differently—and would have if there had been any gain in it.

So perhaps his angle was genuine. On the other hand, he was a very deep one. He could have decided that he might just as well give the inquiry a little support, hold a watching brief and step in if there were any advantage in it for him.

The pilot saw a break above, claimed the space

and accelerated into it. They were in the top lane but one, with intercity traffic moving over at double their speed. There were not many on the upper throughway, mainly freight cars going out to supply bases to collect fresh fruit and vegetables for the morning markets.

Feeling the onus of being the only native in the group, the pilot spoke into his intercom and gave a run-down on the buildings they were passing. A huge illuminated bowl with dazzling green water got a special mention. "Took three years to build. They had to shift a million cubic meters of rock. Those fountains draw from warm springs. There's just about everything on that site—massage rooms, actualizers that set up any scene you can dream, the best food in Argentus. You name it and it's there. If you have a spare day, you couldn't do better than take a look."

Carried away by the thought of it, he twisted around to follow the pleasure dome out of sight and came eyeball to eyeball with Tamar Kelly's dog, which she had balanced on her lap with its feet on the back of his chair.

His startled recoil took him with flailing arms into his console and the car lurched off-course.

At the same time a long black freight car dived without warning from the throughway and appeared in the screen dead ahead. It had seen much service and a gray discoloration on its hull showed that some renewal work was long overdue.

The starboard fender hit a glancing blow and sheared off. The pilot switched to Fingalnian to ease his mind in a long stream of high-pitched comment that needed no transducer as he fought to stop the car going into a lateral spin.

Fletcher had seen an elongated blue-white head through the narrow stern port of the freighter and dived over his table to cannon Tamar Kelly off her squab into the aisle. As they dropped below the coaming every plexiglass port on that side exploded in palm-sized shards and whipped around the cabin.

Gagged by a swath of fine silk hair, Fletcher waited for the crash. His mind evaluated data in cold detachment: height, ground speed, the angle his body told him they were at. His head, taking pressure from a decking rib, was well-placed to gauge the vectors.

Also it would be well-placed to absorb the stress when deceleration was absolute. He reckoned bitterly that it would travel into his sternum.

At the same time, he was aware of his pneumatic landing mat. By reflex her arms had locked around his neck and she was breathing heavily in his left ear, a warm aromatic draught mingled with a strong body scent of sandalwood.

It reminded him that he was not alone in the action. For his own part it had seemed that statistics had caught up. All the times when he should have been dead had loaded the dice. This was the one he couldn't buck.

But then she ought to have a chance.

Mobilizing every ounce of urge to beat the pull, he forced his body to move and clawed a way onto the pilot's squab.

The Fingalnian had rolled clear. Sinclair was out of sight between the seats. The console was hard-edged, brilliant in detail with the broken windshield above it, filled with the rushing detail of a city square coming up as if in a zoom lens.

Feet braced astride on the bulkhead, Fletcher heaved down the double pistol grip for maximum lift and heard the motor scream into overload.

The nose began to rise. Vibration threatened to

shear every rivet in the body shell and the lever was crawling away out of his hand.

Noise through the shattered ports was building to a mind-numbing crescendo, but the nose was still coming up and the square was flattening with an ornate public urinal dead ahead and fifty meters distant.

It would be the last twist of the screw. A terminus of no distinction.

Tamar Kelly had climbed into the space behind him. She was leaning over the back of the squab with her hair streaming away like any Maenad and had her hands over his on the grips.

The lever stopped its forward crawl, hesitated, and then snugged back with a definitive click into maximum gain.

The shuttle clawed up the rococo frontage in a near vertical climb with small trash raining down into the rumble.

Argentus traffic control, getting in on the act, spoke up nastily from the communications panel in agitated Fingalnian.

It was good tense stuff about traffic regs and lane discipline but was lost in the racket of the laboring motor.

The car surged out of the square with traffic in every upper lane scattering as automatic avoidance mechanisms picked up the maverick and went into a spasm. At its ceiling height, twenty meters above the top flight path, Fletcher got it sorted out and cut to level flight.

Noise levels dropped and Argentus control came in loud and clear using speech tones with an emotional overlay. "Taxi Four-Nine-Zero, switch to auto and lock on your recovery beam. Taxi Four-Nine-Zero. Are you receiving me?"

Tamar Kelly's communications training reared its head. She peeled off his back and rolled nimbly over the squab to answer the call. Her fingers were on the switch when Fletcher's voice stopped her dead. "Leave that."

She was used to taking orders from the command island and didn't expect courtesy, but there was a cold shriveling quality in it that had her twisting around to check that she was still with the same man.

First crack out of the box she believed she had shipped with a galactic Jekyll. He was staring ahead, eyes narrowed against the tearing wind, his teeth bared like a dog's.

A hundred meters ahead a black freight shuttle with a spreading gray stain on its counter was keeping station in the metropolitan throughway.

Over and above the noise of the wind through the shattered ports a new sound added its dimension of *angst*. There was the seesaw wail of a police siren coming from every direction at once.

She said reasonably, "Security, commander. They'll nail him good."

It was an invitation to call it a night and let the complaint go through the channels. But Fletcher was locked on to a personal vendetta. Diplomatic usage and long-term interest were out the window. He was fighting a ship-to-ship action with only one overriding priority: to get close enough to use a hand laser on the Scotian rear-end Charley.

The taxi, developing every last erg, tore down onto the slow moving freighter.

Scotian facial geography was not geared to mirror emotion; but the man who appeared at the rear window, in response to an urgent request for information from his pilot who had been watching his

61

scanner, was full of surprise. He had reckoned that the taxi was due, any time at all, to home on the chapel of ease.

To see it skim the top and bear down for an attack on its own account was outside reason. He was slow resighting his heavy duty laser and had only gotten around to taking first pressure when the taxi was ten meters off and seemingly all set to ram the freighter up its carbonized rudder.

Fletcher took a coldly calculated second with his laser cradled on the nook of his left arm and raked into the Scotian from throat to forehead. Then he dropped it at his feet and grabbed for the controls to lift the taxi, at the last possible point in time, over the black hump.

Tamar Kelly aged a little. She had been watching a killer in action and appearances would never be the same again. There was not much time to analyze the situation. Police tenders' sirens iron-tongued had closed up on either quarter.

She tried again: "Security, commander. I think they want to say something."

Fletcher said, "You could be right, communications. Talk to them. Ask them what kind of lane discipline they keep here. Tell them we have a complaint."

The voice was back to normal but the eyes were still bleak. She shivered, suddenly conscious of the cold airstream. Before she could make the call, they had company.

Working in concert, the police tenders extruded flexible grabs to anchor the taxi in a comprehensive grip. Sirens cut abruptly and a detail with a loud hailer spoke the sudden silence.

"Switch off. Move clear of the controls or I shall open fire."

It was a credible threat. Each craft had a marksman with a carbine trained on the shattered cab.

Dave Sinclair heaved himself from between the squabs, shaking his head left and right to check that he still had it whole. His last conscious impression had been of the Fingalnian pilot going into a nervous twitch at the sight of Tamar Kelly's dog and he was full of complaint.

He said, "God save us all. That black misbegotten bastard will do for us yet. Where is it, Kelly? I'll wring its stringy neck."

The Fingalnian spokesman, fearing he was losing his audience, put in another request. "All must sit down with hands on the table."

The composite craft wheeled out of lane with traffic control sorting out a priority path. They homed neatly on the Security Headquarters porch where a long crimson private shuttle was drawn up.

Guards fell in on either side and marched them over to it.

Veck said, "Come in, commander. It is fortunate that I had not already left. As soon as I heard that you were in trouble I decided to wait and talk to you again. I will take you personally to your ship."

He did not speak again until they were airborne. Then he pressed buttons on the arm of his chair to raise an acoustic seal which isolated the two of them from his own pilot and the Sinclair-Kelly duo in the rumble.

"Now perhaps you will believe what I say about the danger in your enterprise. Are you sure there is nothing else you can tell me about the inquiry? Have you no theory at all?"

"You are very quick to assume that we were attacked."

"We are not stupid, commander. Traces of laser

fire were noticed on the hull of the taxi. Also I know enough about you to be sure that you would not involve yourself in an incident without provocation. You must also know however that I have enough grounds to hold you on a civil charge."

"Why don't you do just that?"

"The inquiry you are on may be important to us. I will be frank with you, commander."

Fletcher toyed with the idea of saying, "What, again?" but rejected it and Veck went on: "Subversive elements in Fingalna would like to involve us in a new alignment with O.G.A. The woman Vair was known to belong to such a group. There may be some connection. Do I make myself clear?"

"I can see that you would like to be kept informed. All right. As an I.G.O. representative, I see no harm in that."

"Then we understand each other."

Dag Fletcher reckoned that it was the optimistic statement of all time, but he let it ride. The spaceport was coming into view with *Interstellar X* like an obelisk on her pad. He would settle for getting on board and working it out from there. He would know more about it when he was following *Two Nine*'s last flight path. Until then all the other angles were so much Scotch mist.

As the police car docked at the corvette's main hatch Veck delivered a parting shot. "One piece of information for you, commander. The woman Vair came to Argentus from Croton. She was on the payroll of the Sylea Mining and Manufacturing Company. I have asked myself several times what possible interest such a group could have in an ethnological survey."

64

IV

Circling slowly on his command island, with *Interstellar X* all systems go and Fingalna's green-tinged orb shrinking to a blob in the main scanner, Fletcher had to admit that the problem looked insoluble on the ground.

He should have known that moving his body halfway across the galaxy was no guarantee that all would be made clear. Maybe he had persuaded himself so that he could cut free from his desk, personal restlessness nudging judgment.

At that level at least there was a positive gain. Hulda had receded to a small inset on his mental scanner and her details were blurred. Retroactive inhibition, the headshrinkers called it. One thing after another, with only a confused residue left in the computer. So where did that leave the human spirit? Answer: a self-conscious mollusc reacting instinctively to the environment it had drifted into. One of evolution's limited successes, no more and no less, with no before or after and no abiding point of reference.

Bleeps from a telltale shifted his attention from the star map of a direct vision port to his instrument clusters. The gravisphere of Fingalna had eteliolated to a point where the ship was technically in deep space. Time to stand down. Scullion said, "That wraps it up, commander. Permission to dismiss to quarters."

It was automatic and Hobbs at the communications desk was already methodically stripping seals from his visor.

Fletcher, surrounded by the familiar hardware of

a military unit, was momentarily back in time and slipped into the drill which was standard on a corvette. As outriders of the squadron, they had a duty to see that every arc of vision was clear of visible threat before any crew members stood down from action stations.

He said sharply, "Hold fast, number one. Three-sixty-degree sweep."

Hobbs stopped work on his seals and set his cone receptors for a slow radial scan. Stars wheeled in a random infinite maze across the main scanner.

They could be anywhere and nowhere. The visible galaxy was too big for the human mind to grapple with. And beyond it were others teeming with fantastic life. It was enough to unhinge reason. Perhaps it already had. Maybe he was alone and only imagined the fabric of the starship that carried his thinking eye through this ultimate wilderness.

Hobbs was in the last segment of his sweep through the starboard quarter. A cindery asteroid on an outside orbit around Fingalna showed up like a miniature moon, dark blue with some shimmering iridescence in the tangled spurs of unweathered rock.

Custom-built as an observation satellite, it was strange that the Fingalnians had not put it to use. It would have made a launch platform for a protective fighter screen.

Fletcher said, "Hold fast on that. Close in."

The rough blob expanded to fill the scanner and then peeled away as the probe increased magnification. It could have stood in for anybody's concept of ultimate desolation. They were boring into an empty corner of hell.

There was no gain in it. Fletcher reckoned he would call it a day and jack it in. The words had formed in his head and were on the way to his larynx when Averil Marr's sudden intake of breath hissed through the intercom.

Sitting like a bright tooth in a rotten socket with trails of white gas wreathing all around, a slender ship was preparing for blast-off.

Switching his prepared speech with a change of direction that did his circuitry no good Fletcher snarled, "Retro," and read off the grid lines on the scanner for a fix. Then he was dictating a stream of figures for a course change that brought *Interstellar X* around in a maneuver that no civilian ship could have matched.

Scullion said, "She's moving, commander. We'll be slap on her flight path."

It was a statement of fact and was not contradicted.

Fletcher called Diggory Taft in his gunnery module. "Main beams, navigation two. Everything that bears. Keep it lined up and switch the firing pin to my desk."

At the same time he buzzed Tamar Kelly in her hideout below the cone.

"Communication two to commander."

"Lock onto that ship. Give me distances. Don't stop. Just go on reading them out. Understood?"

"Distances. Understood."

She was giving the first before he had made his next move, a warm steady voice talking into his ear.

Interstellar X began to pick up speed on her new bearing. There was tension in the command cabin that could be felt through the insulation of space gear.

Holdbrook at the power desk said, "That's all you can have, commander. She's full out."

There was space under the rising craft's rocket tubes and a cauldron of vermilion flame spilling out into the jagged wastes of the asteroid.

Seen in full the ship was deadly, brilliantly lacquered with black and yellow stripes on its narrow waist. Now there was no doubt about it. It was a Scotian frigate, a military unit with more firepower in its minor armament than in everything left operational on *Interstellar X*.

Fletcher held on. Tamar Kelly's voice, notched emotionally into a higher register, kept filling his left ear.

It had to be right. He could put himself in the position of the commander of the moving ship. There was a point when it would be possible for him to open fire. Too soon and the recoil would beat his fragile stability and throw him back onto his rocky pad. Too late and he would have given the small corvette its only chance of scoring a hit.

From his own point of view, he wanted maximum damage. There would be no second shot. Once the Scotian was out of his hole, he could stalk *Interstellar X* at his leisure in a chase that could only end one way.

Tamar Kelly's voice was an incredulous squeak. She was watching the action on her bijou scanner and for her money they were on a suicidal collision course. She could imagine Fletcher, grim-faced as he had been in the car, totally absorbed by his purpose, and she wondered what he was really like inside his head.

She called the next whole number reference in the shrinking sequence and it was as though her own voice had triggered off an electric storm. Brilliant streamers of intense light flared across the scanner and enveloped the Scotian ship.

Interstellar X sidestepped bodily and her picture went out of focus. When she had it again, she looked at the grid with open disbelief and had to check that she was in the right area.

The asteroid was there, still smoldering with molten slag from the blastoff, but the ship had gone except for a glowing nimbus, an electric haze that still held the notional shape of a starship.

Rising gee sank her to the depths of her acceleration couch. The asteroid dipped abruptly out of vision. Fletcher had pulled clear over the glowing gas cloud that marked the position in space and time lately filled by the Scotian.

Two minutes later his voice was coming over the intercom on an all-hands call. "The course is Croton. Normal watch. Stand down."

A less sensitive man than Fletcher would have picked up the mood of the ship's company. *Interstellar X* was plumb on course, sliding like a bobbin on the thread her computers had spun out to link her with the control tower of Breseus spaceport on the forty-third parallel of Croton. Watch followed watch with clockwork precision and every department ran smooth as oiled machinery under Scullion's direction. But underlying all was a reservation. They had not signed for a hot war.

There was also the unspoken opinion that he had broken a foundation rule in the deep-space code. Life was held on a fragile thread. More than any other people, those who joined the profession had a personal knowledge of it. There was a kinship among starfarers of every culture. To destroy another ship was a kind of sacrilege.

Even Taft who had some military experience had not been in that kind of action.

Fletcher accepted it. The essential loneliness of command was no novelty to him. In a way he valued them more for it. But he reckoned he could have done no other.

Coupled with the other personal attempts to delay the mission, he knew beyond the reach of reason that the Scotian had been sited there as an interceptor. He was right, but there was no proof.

With the corvette running on a minimum crew list, he stood watch as a navigator to relieve Scullion and Averil Marr. Crewmen were correct and in no way hostile, but free conversation died the death when he toook his seat on the command island.

Illogically, he found himself more concerned when the duty roster brought him on watch with Sinclair at the power desk and Tamar Kelly at communications. They moved about with elaborate caution as if they expected him to go off in a berserker phase any minute. Tamar Kelly kept her dog out of sight as though some things were too shocking for its pure eye to see.

As far as he could judge there had been no report of the incident. Routine messages came out relayed from Fingalna. Nothing about a missing ship. There was a brief session with Spencer on the scrambled two-way link.

It had cost a fortune and the chairman used a few valuable seconds to say so. News of the trouble in Fingalna had reached him and he wanted confirmation. Talking fast in the interest of economy he also said, "Hear this. If you decide that there's more to this than an accident, I want you out. Leave it to I.G.O. God knows we pay enough in taxes. I want that ship here in one piece. Also I have schedules to meet. I need you and your crew. Do the survey. Make a report and get back. Is that clear?"

Fletcher said, "There's one thing you can do for me, chairman. Get word to Admiral Frazer. Ask if he knows that there was a Scotian frigate based on an asteroid on the Fingalnian perimeter. If he has any information I'd like to hear from him. Either at Croton or Bromius."

"So you're going to Croton?"

"In and out. Then Bromius. On the way I'll follow Walker's flight path. I can refuel in Bromius, miss out Fingalnia and run straight for home."

"Well watch it, I know you. Don't go out of line."

At the watch change Scullion, Holdbrook and Randle Hobbs took over the desks. Sinclair, with less to transfer in the middle passage when the power was cut back to a whisper from the mercury ion subsidiary motors, was away first. Then Tamar Kelly.

As Fletcher cleared with his copilot and swung himself through the hatch, he met her on a return trip.

The narrow companion was basically for one-way traffic and she flattened herself against the bulkhead to make room.

Fletcher said, "What is it then? Haven't you had enough?"—and it sounded banal in his own ears.

One part of his mind was judging that when in a womblike tube and squeezing past a taut redhead wearing a white inner suit that fitted like a sheath there ought to be something else to say.

Brown candid eyes ten centimeters off were considering him and seemed to have knowledge of what was going on in his head. She knew that he was not satisfied with what he had said and also knew that he knew she knew.

It was like a mirror progression in depth. They stopped for a second longer than the passage should have taken to consider it.

71

Tamar Kelly saw the hard brown face as though for the first time and wanted to ask how he had come by the radiation burn that drew his left eyebrow into a quizzical lift. She actually said, "I forgot my lucky dog. He's in the equipment locker. I wouldn't like Randy to pull him out thinking his leg was a filing tube."

She had not said what she meant either. Honors were even in social deceit and they were past with tactile data to store in the holographic web of memory and a sense of unfinished business.

Plainer speaking was going on in an alcove of the passenger terminal at Breseus spaceport. Sited where they could watch the illuminated star map which showed craft in passage on the spacelanes as bright moving counters, an ill-assorted couple were locked in a quiet wrangle.

A bulky Laodamian built on the ground plan of an Earth-type gorilla was using a sophisticated transducer to talk to a Scotian.

He said, "The Earth ship will leave rationalized time and enter this gravisphere within twelve hours local reckoning. You said it was taken care of. What has happened to your ship?"

A muted rattle from the Scotian's vocalizer sorted itself into, "I do not know."

"What kind of answer is that? My superior and yours will want more than that."

The Scotian's tongue licked redly around his leather mouth. Some of the menace was filtered out by the gear, but there was enough left to remind the Laodamian that even a technical expert was replaceable. Scotians were dangerous allies. "Take care. I will answer for my part. How can I know what has happened? My commander has reason for what he

72

does. But it is clear from the chart that the Earth ship will arrive at this port. Make the signal. There will be other instructions. When you have them you know where to find me."

The Scotian uncoiled his lean two-meter length, stared stonily at the display board and walked out without a backward glance.

His partner shrugged, slipped the apparatus into a sling pack and crossed the lobby to a line of video booths. When his number answered he said briefly, "Personal line to Director Scarphe," and fished in his useful bag for another gadget. When he had it fixed over the mouthpiece of the handset he waited for the director's all-clear to show up.

A black double helix glowed on the screen. He said, "Pemptus, director. There has been some mistake. The Earth ship has not been destroyed. It is approaching Croton."

"Wait."

Pemptus watched the busy traffic in the reception area: mainly dark-skinned Crotonians with a sprinkling of nationals from every planet in the outer quarter.

An unconsidering observer would have classed him as an aboriginal put on exhibition in a glass case. He or she would have been wildly wrong. The Laodamians had forgotten more about personality engineering than most cultures would ever know. They were the technocrats of the galaxy and had kept life viable on their small cooling planet when reason would have said there was no future in it. Over the last century more and more had opted out and found employment elsewhere in bitterness of spirit, feeling themselves superior to their hosts but never being accepted as equals.

They had a tendency to drift into ventures which

were lined up to disrupt the state, as if the spread of anarchy were the only satisfaction left.

Nobody shoved a banana through the lock, but Pemptus shifted uneasily about his cage as though he expected it any minute.

The video cracked into life. Scarphe said, "Further instructions will be sent to you. Meanwhile, find out where the commander of the Earth ship will stay. Record all conversations he has. I want to know what he intends to do and what information he has. A courier will collect your reports at the usual place every six hours as from now. Is that understood?"

It was as well that the visual link was not in use. Pemptus's lips writhed back from his massive choppers in a mirthless grin. His voice, however, was all gentle compliance, a soft melodious job, out of key with the savage ape face. "That is understood, director. Of course it will be costly. The equipment is very specialized. There is also the personal risk. The law in Croton is very strict on unauthorized surveillance. For you, because I appreciate your purposes, I will do this for twenty dacrons an hour."

The unseen Crotonian was also protected by the blank screen. Tall and well-preserved, but with hair showing streaks of white that showed he was old in Crotonian reckoning, he switched himself off the speech link and shared his judgment with a Bromusian girl who was lying on his office sofa. "These monkeys are all the same, Fanchon. They have only one thing to sell and they push for a high price. This one is asking twenty dacrons an hour and hinting that he knows I cannot refuse."

"Why not give it to me? I could find out all you want to know for that kind of money."

"You already cost too much."

Scarphe released the button and said, "I prefer to

74

pay by results. Ten as a fee and the rest as I value the results."

"Twenty, director."

"Fifteen and a bonus if your information is useful."

"Twenty, director. The risk is the same whether the information is useful or not."

"Very well. See that you do a good job."

Fanchon swung long slim legs off the sofa and stretched like a cat. "The monkey made a good deal."

"He will not gain by it. As soon as this business is finished, he will be taken care of."

"All the same you should have let me go. Earthmen are very naive and trusting. Because we are like them they think that our minds work the same way. They are children."

She stood up and walked with a sinuous wiggle to his long observation window. Long black hair brushed silkily to the first lumbar vertebra of her bare back intensified the ivory pallor of her smooth skin.

No prude, but conscious of public relations, Scarphe said, "Bromusian customs are out of place here. Put your sari on. The work force is already unsettled enough."

"We manage things better in Bromius. Everybody keeps in station and there is no discontent. It is very undignified to care what your workers think. Also we have methods to smooth out unwelcome ideas."

Scarphe said irritably, "Just do it. I have enough to worry about." He sat down behind his desk and tapped it with a stylus while she made a small houri's epic of doing her master's bidding.

Distracted by it, he lowered his mental guard and allowed her in on the e.s.p. link. It was another Bromusian trait that was difficult to live with.

She said, "You worry too much. The Earthman has been lucky. Statistics are against him. This time

75

he will be stopped. In any case he cannot find out what happened to his ship."

Scarphe belatedly put up his barrier and fairly snapped, "Take a car and go to the lido. I'll join you in an hour. Keep your fingers out of my head or you'll find that there are simple methods even in Croton to deal with busy-minded drabs."

"Temper, temper. I'm only trying to help."

"Get out."

At the door she said, "Think about it. If you change your mind, I'm serious. I will go to Breseus and meet the starship."

"Just walk up to the commander and say you're a special welcome service."

"As a matter of fact I know a Bromusian girl who was on some kind of mission with him. She came from my commune. Very earnest. In the I.G.O. service. That would be introduction enough."

"As you say, I'll think about it. As of now do me a favor and do as I say."

When she had gone, Scarphe selected keys from the cluster that filled one side of his desk. A robot secretary began to speak quietly into his ear and illustrative data appeared as a flowing diagram on the left-hand wall of his luxury office. It was all bad news. Without a radical change in the I.G.O. quota of infrangom ore, his plant would be working on half-capacity before the end of the month. And the forecast was worse. Either he had to increase his supplies or modify the industrial complex for some other process.

He had seen that happen before. It was a long and dispiriting process with no guarantee of success at the end of it. For himself, at age sixty, there was no time. He wanted something that would work out in the last decade of his active control. That was what the plan promised. He would end in a blaze of success with proconsular power over an expanded empire.

It was worth the risk. Soon the politicians would make their open moves. Then he could opt out of the intrigue bit and get back to the industrial angle he knew.

Fletcher conned his ship on manual for the last phase of planetfall.

It was something to do to keep his mind off his problems and the best possible exercise to integrate with his crew in a maneuver where they were all dependent on each other and in the last analysis on himself.

Not that he wanted applause. But he reckoned they should know that it could be done and they would have that much more confidence in the ship in case there were any other finely run enterprise.

To some extent it payed off. Every desk was shoved to the limit of its human operator as Fletcher's flat steady voice called for data.

He was seeing the vectors as a three-dimensional diagram in his head with the ship as a moving rod. It was a fantastic exhibition of expertise.

When *Interstellar X* hit the pad and flexed precisely to the limit of her hydraulic jacks, there was a sigh of unconsciously released tension. They had made it, much as early navigators crossed an unknown sea—by their own efforts.

Scullion said, "Holy cow. That was something," and was speaking for all hands.

Fletcher said, "One thing. I don't expect to stay long in Breseus. Arrangements as before. Working nucleus on the ship at all times. Otherwise short local trips within one hour radius of the port. I need hardly say there must be no mention of the Scotian. I shall make a report of that to I.G.O. Don't even discuss it among yourselves. They have some very refined listening beams in this part of the world. Well done, all."

He had Diggory Taft break out the patrol car and was moving off with the I.G.O. pennant streaming stiffly in the airflow before the gray coolant had cleared from the pad.

On the way from his cabin he had seen Tamar Kelly and Sinclair in close session in the ward room. They would be on the same relief detail and were no doubt fixing some shared scheme of pleasure. His mind allowed the half-formed thought to pass that he should have got Scullion to put them on different watches. But he did not pursue the idea to its seed bed in the unconscious anthill where motivation had its nest.

The port controller, a dark-faced Crotonian, appeared in person as a courtesy gesture to an I.G.O. official. A lapel tab identified him as Executive Pemon and his voice colored all he said with the harmonic of a permanent gripe. But the form of words was civil enough. "You made a good passage, commander. I see from your manifest that you will only make a short stay. It is a long way to come for such a brief visit. Your business must be important."

Fletcher marveled at it. The man must know why he was there. Maybe he wanted to play it along as though there was no suggestion from the Croton end that anything out of the way had happened to *Two Nine*.

"I am investigating the loss of a starship. You will be as anxious as I am to protect the safety of the spacelanes."

"That is so, of course, commander. You will be

referring to *Interstellar Two Nine*. If the ship had been routed from here we would have mounted an inquiry ourselves. But as you know it did not come here. As far as we know her commander changed his mind and altered course for some other destination. How can I help you?"

"I would like to see the log of the conversation with the ship."

"Of course. It is very brief. Just a preliminary signal, you understand. We had not taken charge for a controlled planetfall. I believe he asked for data for a proving orbit, which was given together with acceptance into this gravisphere. He appeared to change course for such an orbit; Then, as I say, his plans were altered. But then, you commanders have your own methods. You yourself came in without pilotage. Very expertly, of course. But it is a danger-ous practice. Frankly I would welcome a regulation that compelled all ships to accept course control from the tower."

Pemon flipped in his video and spoke on a direct line to his operations room: "Search out the record of exchanges with the Earth starship *Interstellar Two Nine* and play it through to me."

He left his desk, touched a panel on his office wall and a white screen unfolded.

"While we are waiting, is there anything else I can help you with?"

"Just one thing. What do you know of the Sylea Industrial Complex?"

There could have been a hesitation and a quick saccadic eye movement, but it was fractional and Pemon's voice had no special emphasis as he said, "That is in the north. Two hours by an intercon-tinental shuttle. Most of our industry is concen-trated in that region. A very tidy arrangement. The

Sylea complex deals with infrangom—which as you will know is regulated by I.G.O. inspection. I know nothing of it except that it is regarded as one of the key structures in our economy. What has this to do with the loss of your ship?"

Fletcher was saved an immediate answer. A warning bleep from the screen area prefaced the beginning of a transmission. The screen glowed blue and then darkened into a familiar star map. A tiny moving point of light showed *Interstellar Two Nine* entering the gravisphere of Croton.

Croton control spoke using speech tones and Neil Walker answered. There was nothing new. It was exactly what he had heard before on the flight record.

Hearing it again from the Croton end, however, there was a definite feeling that Walker had intended to come in. There was no reason at all why he should not have. It was not by choice.

The bright dot on the screen broke from the long curve of its calculated path and slanted out until it blanked on the perimeter of Croton space.

"You see commander. It is no fault of ours. There was no damage signal or appeal for help."

"How often does it happen that a ship enters your space and then sheers off?"

"Often enough."

"Every day?"

"Not every day, of course, but often enough not to cause any special alarm. In any case, what could we have done? Croton is not a space power. We do not have an interceptor screen or any standby craft that could overtake a starship."

Fletcher let it go. He took a solitary meal in the spaceport diner and then made a call on the Earth Consulate which was sited in the admin complex.

McStein, the resident, was an Armenian, a dapper ageless type with liquid brown eyes and expressive hands.

"I know no more than you, commander. This is a small department, you understand, and I have many other interests. I act as local factor for certain patents and copyright interests. At the time, I was in the southern region capital on a business trip. There was no reason for me to be involved."

"But you knew about the expedition. Dr. Izod was proposing to do a survey. He must have contacted you about that."

"If asked of course I would make local arrangements for a party from Earth. But in this case there was direct negotiation with the Ministry of the Interior."

"You have a record of Earth nationals on Croton?"

"Yes, but there is no guarantee that it is complete. I am here to help, but there is no regulation that says every visitor from our planet must register with the consulate."

"Could I see it?"

"Certainly, commander."

McStein spoke into the left ear of a pot nymph on his desktop. "Briggita, pass in the visitor's file for Commander Fletcher."

That was the first item that sounded an offbeat note for Fletcher's delicate receptors. Why specify for whom? What was Briggita to him or he to Briggita that she should need to know his name?

When she came in, walking with small steps on high-heeled sandals, platinum hair in a high-coiled pagoda, she was literally revealed as a small delicate Fingalnian with a hexagonal navel jewel and a wisp of translucent bolero.

She said, "Here it ith, Matt. Do you want anything elth?"

"Not as of now. Take any calls and say I'll call back later."

She teetered out with an ambience of ankle bells and McStein, following Fletcher's surprised eye, said, "Earth staff don't stay. I find local labor more satisfactory. Continuity is the great thing, commander. If *you* need a secretary while you are here, I am sure I can find you one."

He handed over the file without looking at it and Fletcher had an intuition that he would find no mention of Reina Vair in its nominal roll.

It was short enough and would not overtax Briggita to keep it up to date. There were sixty-three Earth nationals on Croton, mostly in Breseus itself and attached to subsidiaries of commercial companies. There were only two women listed as buyers for couture houses. Reina Vair was not among them.

"Was there some particular person you had in mind?"

"Just a longshot. I understood that Dr. Izod's party included a woman called Vair who had once been resident in Croton."

"The name means nothing to me."

Fletcher stood up to go. "It looks like a dead end. Thank you anyway for your help."

"Not at all, commander. That is why I am here." His face was filled to its last square centimeter with an obliging smile, all white teeth and sincerity.

At the door Fletcher said, "I want to call on the Sylea Industrial Complex. Is there any problem?"

The smile died the death. McStein said, "It is a restricted area. You will have to make application."

"That's all right. You do it for me. It shouldn't be too difficult, I have I.G.O. diplomatic status. I'll be at the port hotel. Sometime before the end of the day. Your secretary can fix a seat on a shuttle. Don't take no for an answer."

Pemptus locked on to Fletcher's unique pattern of brain currents and, following his progress with refined tuning, keyed in a time and place reference and slipped a new microwire into his monitor.

Delicate fingers, out of phase with his uncouth bulk, took the used spiral and fed it gently into the cellulose filter of a cigarette which he returned to its pack.

Fletcher's computer was off-load and throwing up random imagery. The Laodamian sucked his massive teeth and wrinkled his ape nose. That was a development now that they should work on. It would add a lot to the interest of a monitoring chore if he could actually see into the subject's head. There was a legend that his people had once gotten that far, but the knowledge had been lost centuries back in the global troubles that had finally shifted Laodamia out of the big league of galactic powers.

Now they were the electronic tinkers of the spaceways, thrown commissions like scraps.

It was half an hour before he had anything to record and he enjoyed the ironic twist in it.

A Fingalnian, probably female, had come into Fletcher's magnetic field. She said, "The Conthul thent me to find you, commander. The arrangementth are made. Here ith your rethervation on the fourteen hundred thutle. The director of the Thylea Completkh will meet you at the terminal. He ith called Thcaphe."

V

Seen from the IBS in a brief flash before it flipped base over tip and wreathed itself in a flare of retro, Sylea Industrial Complex was spread out on a vast triangular plain, bounded by a wide sluggish river, a freight monorail on pylons and the long straight scar of an old surface road that ran along the top of an embankment.

It looked like reclaimed land. Maybe at some point in Croton history there had been an inland sea on the site.

A wheeled toastrack with a blue-and-white striped awning carried human freight from the pad to a circular reception tower flying the house flag of the corporation, a double black helix on a white ground.

The same symbol was repeated in ground glass on the double-leaf transparent doors. In fact it seemed to be carried out on every artifact on the set. The company was a private empire and Fletcher reckoned that the personnel were lucky not to have it branded on either cheek.

A tall man getting deference from all hands made a royal progress across the lobby and intercepted him before he reached the inquiry desk.

"You will be Commander Fletcher."

It was a fair basis for agreement, but the man pushed on with his own good news. "I am Director Scarphe. This way, commander."

A long luxurious car heavy on gold trim and flying the company pennant from the apex of its plexidome was waiting at a private porch. Two men in uniform, with equipment harness and short carbines on shoulder straps, opened the doors and then sat side by side in the rujmble.

The pilot, isolated in his cockpit by a wall-to-wall glass panel, watched the embussing through his mirror and took off as soon as they were all in.

After his first burst of bonhomie Scarphe had not spoken and a new voice took up the burden.

It surprised Fletcher, because he had not registered that there was other company. When he turned to check it out, he was only centimeters distant from a Bromusian girl who had uncurled from the squab behind him and was leaning elegantly forward to communicate to his left ear.

For a moment his mind gagged. It was as though Hulda had materialized out of the woodwork. The face was near enough the same to be an identical twin and the voice had the same Bromusian timbre. But the content was wrong and this one had jet-black hair clinging damply like a shiny skullcap.

"So you are the famous Commander Fletcher. I thought you would have been much older."

"Older than what?"

"Don't be like that. It was a compliment. I am Franchon." A slim hand appeared over the backrest and again he was reminded of Hulda by its texture. She held on longer than was necessary and continued with, "What brings you to this grim corner of Croton?"

Fletcher was suddenly on-guard. He remembered Hulda's talent for e.s.p. This one was talking to focus his mind her way and could be digging around even now. He deliberately cleared his head of every conscious thought and answered by free association.

Confirmation came as she leaned back with a shadow of disappointment that she was not quick enough to hide.

"Grim? It looks very comfortable. You have it all buttoned up, director."

"We try to be efficient. But your organization does not help with its restrictive quotas."

"There's a big queue for strategic materials. In a free-for-all you could get less."

"Or a great deal more."

The quick dusk of Croton was rolling in like a dark tidal wave and lights flared automatically from all parts of the complex. They were passing a small manmade mountain with a long slab of coke ovens on its flat top. Small figures of men moving on gantries were thrown into silhouette. There was a brilliant narrow oblong of vermilion laced with cadmium yellow as a hopper collected a full due from an open section.

"The plant is still working at least."

"There would be expensive damage if it stopped. But it is hardly economic to continue with the volume of production at present. Are you interested in the process?"

Fletcher reckoned he could have made a tour of an infrangom plant on Earth, but then, if the man were anxious to do a P.R. job for his product, he should be encouraged. "As a consumer I should know how it all begins."

Scarphe pulled a handset from a niche on his armrest and spoke rapidly in Crotonian to the pilot.

The car veered from an illuminated guide strip on the tarmac below and followed the dark bulk of a huge isolated building that appeared to glow from some intense inner light.

They pulled in beside a row of ore trucks and Scarphe slipped back the hatch. Heat flooded in. A gauge over the lintel climbed to twenty-five Celsius.

Scarphe said, "A furnace is being tapped. One of

the highlights of the sequence. If we hurry along you should catch it."

They ducked through a low door into a checkpoint where there was instant activity as soon as the director's face came into the light: more rapid gobbledegook, and white coveralls were zipped out of fresh sterile packs and handed out.

Fletcher noted that the two guards took turns to seal up so that one was at the ready with his carbine handy for use at all times. It spoke well for the semimilitary discipline of the outfit.

Fanchon made a striptease of the exercise, bringing a boudoir touch to the industrial scene. Director Scarphe, a quick dresser, was already standing on the threshold of an elevator cage as she put in a last lithe wriggle and got herself cantilevered to present the double helix on her breast pocket at an optimum angle.

The cage rose for a hundred meters and decanted them in a semicircular glass bubble that projected over the working area and held a horseshoe console which controlled the action.

Seen from the inside, the building looked too big to be the work of men. Lost in distance either way, spidery gantries ran like a web in every direction. A rolling cloud of white gas, lit redly from below, was hiding the high roof. A two-meter-wide tongue of incandescent metal was thrusting out from the side of a massive furnace and splashing into a cone-shaped mold.

Scarphe walked rapidly around the horseshoe without speaking to the half-dozen seated operators.

Then he led them over to a blister at the side of the dome and Fletcher recognized all the earmarks of an atmosphere lock. Having stepped often enough through its counterpart into deep space, he reckoned there would be nothing to surprise him. But when the outer door slid away, he had to concede that he was wrong on all counts.

Noise level escalated out of all proportion to the simple act. Noise and heat both, with an acrid sulphurous stench that gripped nose, throat and eyes in a concerted attack.

Scarphe was already moving out on a narrow catwalk and he followed blindly, feeling a pneumatic nudge as Fanchon closed up.

Noise was the greatest hazard. It hammered every idea flat. He remembered a well-documented research item which had proved that as noise increased an operator abandoned task refinement and concentrated on a minimum number of main issues. That figured. It occurred to him that number one on his own list was to stay alive.

Scarphe had reached a platform seemingly clewed by sky bolts to middle space and directly above the eye-aching cauldron. He leaned on the rail and pointed down, eyes screwed to a slit to reduce glare.

Audio clues were out, swamped in the phrenetic clatter from all sides, but personal radar was working for Fletcher. Fanchon had lined up on the rail leaving a meter slot for him to fill. A sensitive crawl of nerves down his back told him that the two guards were close. There could be nothing planned, because he had more or less invited himself on the tour. But if Scarphe was an opportunist it was all set up for as neat an accident as could be arranged.

He could even see the text of the dispatch. "The I.G.O. envoy asked to see the furnace being tapped. He appeared to be overcome by the noise and the fumes and fell from the platform before any of the party could reach him."

Fanchon turned from the rail smiling like a cream-fed cat. She was on circuit and had read the text with him. Eyes dark, with distended pupils, she was endorsing it as a probable course of action.

Dag Fletcher moved into the slot left vacant for him and then sidestepped smartly, crowding the girl into her corner of the platform. One of the guards, arms straight from the shoulder, palms flat for the push, ploughed past, hit the rail with his navel and went into free-fall like any high-board diver.

There was a moment of balance, a still tableau: Fanchon feeling the baluster grinding into her back, Scarphe open-mouthed watching the white figure accelerate under gravity toward the brilliant disk of the mold, and the remaining guard checked in midpace holding out one hand as though in warning.

Fletcher was first away, shoving off from his pneumatic reredos for a sprint start. He had the guard's carbine by the barrel and heaved down with the shoulder strap as a fulcrum.

The heavy butt, following simple mechanical law, swept in a tight arc and homed on the back of the head with a force that shot his peaked hat off. Given the noise level it was all strictly silent comedy, but there was no doubt about the payoff. His knees buckled and Fletcher had to give him room to fall.

Scarphe had not moved. He was watching a small eruption in the molten infrangom. The girl was pounding at his rigid arm for attention. He straightened slowly as Fletcher joined them holding the carbine by its strap.

A good metallurgist, he looked shocked; he clearly thought the sample had all the adulteration it could take. His mime for Fletcher not to drop the carbine over the sidet was a classic in is field.

Down below a number of blue lights had gone into a rhythmic blink to warn all hands that there was an emergency on. It was late for the guard but could serve to orientate his departing ka for an exit from the confusion. Antlike figures had appeared on the lower catwalks.

Fletcher did a little mime of his own, pointing for Scarphe to go first on the return trip and reinforced it by a banner headline: "You too, Delilah."

Fanchon picked it up but looked puzzled. Direction was, however, clear enough and she was first to the catwalk, with Scarphe automatically following and Fletcher bringing up the rear.

When the outer door of the lock closed behind them and there was sudden silence, Fletcher spoke into it. "An appalling thing, director. Do you have many accidents like that? The other man tried to stop him and clubbed himself with his carbine. What would make a man do a thing like that? Noise and heat, I suppose, could unhinge him."

It was crude, but it was a formula. If Scarphe accepted it, he was guilty as hell. If he didn't he had some explaining to do anyway.

Fanchon, more suggestible or more subtle, saw it as a working compromise. She said, "The mind is on a knife edge, commander. Who will ever know?"

With time to think, Scarphe had decided to go along with the politic lie at least for a season. Also he must have recognized that the technical staff in the dome were no match for the Earthman who was carrying the carbine in the crook of his arm with one finger casually lined up on the firing stud.

He would have to wait for time to tie his hands. He said, "I am sorry your visit should have been marred by such an accident. We have a good record here.

Fatalities are very rare. And it is not easy work as you have seen."

Work had stopped in the dome. Every eye tracked them in. They were waiting for a signal. Scarphe spoke to the right-hand marker: "Call casualty. Tell them to send a stretcher up here. Mermeron is on the platform. He tried to catch the man who fell and hurt his head on a stanchion. I shall be in my office for the next hour."

There was more room in the elevator, but less comfort. It was a prickly ride with even Fanchon gone quiet and looking sulky.

At ground level, the anteroom had filled up with security details drawn from all parts of the plant by the all-stations alert. Scarphe, conscious that he was first in line for any hot war, said, "There is nothing to be done. Return to normal working. I shall be in my office for a time. There was no negligence. The company accepts responsibility."

In the car he said, "We have a very generous scheme for compensation. It makes for a contented labor force."

Fletcher said, "I have already taken up a lot of your time. As you may know, I am investigating the loss of one of my company's ships. As a starting point I want to check on the personnel who were aboard. Dr. Izod's secretary once worked for you and I would like your observations on the sort of person she was. It is simply a matter of trying to rule out any possibility that the ship was hijacked, you understand."

"Who was this? There is only a small turnover. Staff usually stay for a term of years."

As a *mot juste*, "turnover" fitted Reina Vair. The small jest appeared on Fletcher's mental retina and Fanchon shrugged as though she thought it were too feeble for an adult mind to give houseroom to.

Warned that she was digging in his head again, Fletcher concentrated on a picture of the absent blonde, hoping for some faint sign of recognition. But the Bromusian was either too clever or had never seen her, so he put it into overt speech. "A tall blonde girl. Unmistakable, I would say. Name of Reina Vair."

Reply from Scarphe was a shade too prompt. "No, commander. The name means nothing to me. Nor the description. But this is a big concern, we have many thousands on the payroll. You can check the records from my office. It looks as though your long journey has been wasted."

In the office, watched by Fanchon from her sofa which she settled on like a homing pigeon, Scarphe played the tapes on his pianola. Fletcher scrutinized a flip-through of all female staff employed by the Sylea Company for a decade.

They were an interesting cosmopolitan lot: silvery Fingalnians; pale-skinned Bromusians; Crotonians who could have been the same girls shown in negative; three Earth-types who could not have been Reina Vair with any cosmetic camouflage; and isolated entries from all planets within the commercial circle of Croton.

Running at ten a minute, it took half an hour by the clock before the screen blanked. Halfway through Fanchon, looking bored, moved to a point behind the director's console and then drifted casually off through an internal door to another part of the forest. As the last picture winked out, Scarphe said, "There it is, commander. She does not appear to be among them, even under a different name."

"Do you have a visitors' file?"

"For official visitors, trade delegations and the like, yes."

"Can I see that?"

Scarphe hesitated. "That is classified information. In the commercial sense only, that is. It is not always advisable to broadcast information about who our customers are. Infrangom is a strategic material."

"It will take me about ten minutes to get a directive from the I.G.O. consul in Breseus. You can do it then or now."

For the third time in almost as many minutes, Scarphe's eyes flicked to the ornate time disk on his office wall. Either he wanted his dinner or he was expecting something to mature.

Fletcher suddenly missed Fanchon. With her e.s.p. linkages, she could have gotten an unspoken brief and gone to carry it out.

Still, there was nothing much he could do about it.

Scarphe came to a decision, maybe conditioned by the thought that the information would never be used. "Very well, commander. I will trust your discretion. Taking the same period of time, there will be more to see because they are not separated into male and female. Perhaps you will accept a higher speed?"

"Just push them along."

Notched up to one a second, the succession of faces became a bizarre dream sequence.

It was like a single face changing slowly in time-lapse, shortening, rounding out, hair receding or growing shoulder-length. Underlying all was the basic human skull with eyes staring out on the world trying to do the sum and find an identity.

Running into the current year, there was a patch when the face seemed to stick on a repeating loop with such small change that for a count of twenty it could have been the same sitter: elongated, blue-white, reptilian with eye disks that stared beadily into the lens.

Fletcher called a halt. "That's a big party. Scotians. What would Scotians want with trade? They only have an armament industry and they're outside the I.G.O. trading network."

"There is peace between the planets of the Rim and I.G.O. We are encouraged to make trade links wherever possible. Scotia is no exception. You will find that the visit was authorized by the Economic Ministry. There was no secret about it."

"It is a large party."

"I think you must leave the management of this company to me, commander. That is not your concern."

Scarphe's voice had suddenly taken a firmer timbre. Before he spoke he had taken another look at his clock.

It all added up to a warning. Fletcher suddenly knew for a truth that he had stayed too long in one place. The opposition had been given time to mount a counterstroke. Probably nothing too well-documented, but the girl knew the score and would know the operating channels.

He stood up and walked to the long observation window. Scarphe's empire was lost in gloom except for ribbons of brightly lit roadway and the beacon glare of the coke plant, on its artificial mountain.

As he watched two long shuttles appeared out of darkness and went to ground under the canopy of the porch.

He could see Scarphe at his desk reflected in the glass, twisting a long paperknife in his fingers. Without turning around he asked, "Was Reina Vair attached to the Scotian delegation?"

Involuntary reflex tightened the Crotonian's grip

on his therapy object and it arched suddenly in a curve that tested its tensile strength to the limit. He answered too quickly, "Why do you say that? Surely you are satisfied, commander, that your Reina Vair has never visited this plant. I cannot speak for the rest of Croton, of course. But you should pursue your inquiries elsewhere. I have been very patient. But you must understand I am not without influence on this planet and I intend to report your persistent refusal to accept my good faith to your superiors."

Fletcher said coldly, "That is up to you of course." He turned from the window. There was, anyway, nothing more to see, but he was conscious that a posse could now be making its way up through the tower block. He went on: "I hope you are acting in good faith. If you are not, be sure that I.G.O. will get around to it. I am just asking questions about a civil accident, a legitimate and necessary exercise. If it should turn out to be anything else there will be an I.G.O. taskforce in Croton space. The safety of the spacelanes is I.G.O. business. Make no mistake about that."

A blue telltale flicked into life on Scarphe's console and he picked up a handset. "All that is very interesting, commander. Excuse me a moment."

What he heard seemed to do him good. Eyes fairly snapping with the dark pleasure of malice, he said, "Very good, you have done well. Anytime now," into his intercom and, to Fletcher, "This interview is concluded, commander. You will find a car waiting to take you to the terminal."

It was out of character. He was putting himself in personal danger. First crack out of the bag a suspicious opponent would insist on company for the trip. And Fletcher was still carrying the carbine on his shoulder.

Still smiling, Scarphe replaced the handset and shoved over a small key beside it.

Before Fletcher could cross the four meters of parquet between them the room had divided itself into two self-contained units. Scarphe and his desk and private exit were sealed off by a transparent arc of shiny glass that dropped from the roof and homed on a shallow gulley with a definitive click.

Like any prudent industrialist Scarphe had gotten himself set with a protective screen in case the peasantry got it up its nose and forced an audience. His voice came from an external speaker, reinforcing the message: "Goodbye, commander."

It was indeed time to go. Past the politic time more than likely. Fletcher prodded the screen with the butt of the carbine and said, "One word of warning, director. Scotians never made a two-way contract yet. Don't count on their support if the going gets rough. And believe me, if you have it in mind to sidestep I.G.O. requirements, it will get very rough. I'll be seeing you again in the fullness of time."

Scarphe's smile from inside his aquarium had no element of humor in it.

Fletcher took the outer door to the landing and stood with his back to it, weighing up the angles. The area was lush with potted plants and one wall at his left housed a ten-meter tank full of bubbles and busy fish. Dead ahead, there was a stairhead for a narrow spiral staircase carried in a transparent tube that ran up like a column to the penthouse. To the right there was a door marked DEPUTY DIRECTOR and a double elevator trunk.

Telltales flicking in sequence on the nearer elevator showed that a cage was on the way up. Even as he watched, the score was complete and a wall strip lit up with some legend in Crotonian that could only mean, "It's here, mate."

As the door began to slice open he unshipped the carbine and aimed chest-high for the widening gap. It was empty. He was being invited to take a ride.

His own action was warning enough. He could imagine the cage homing on the ground floor with a reception party fanned out in a darkened foyer and himself brilliantly lit as a competition target.

The centerpiece of the floral display was a jardiniere on castors for ease of deployment. It carried a sunflower variant in a bronze urn—a massive plate-sized white heart with vermilion petals. He shouldered the carbine and trundled it forward. As soon as its weight hit the platform, there was a soft melodious bleep and auto gear began to operate the inner door. On a count of three the cage was all buttoned up and accelerating away for its R.V.

Fletcher padded silently across to the staircase. They were expecting him to go down, which was anyway the only logical way to get out, so he would go up.

On the next floor he was at journey's end. There was a small landing and no ongoing spiral. The penthouse itself, opening off through a Moorish arch, was a large conservatory area dimly lit by courtesy lights and floored with a thick purple carpet and a scattering of huge circular yellow cushions like so many lilypads on a wine-dark pool. Fanchon's playpen for a gold clock.

He put his ear flat to the elevator trunk. The muted whine of the gear suddenly cut off. The cage had reached base. In his mind's eye he could see the door slicing away. There was a rhythmic thump which needed no gloss.

Even though it was what he had known by intuition, the reality of it was something else. They had not waited to identify him or give him time to adjust to a terminal situation. A volley had torn into the cage and cut the sunflower down in its prime.

Another thought struck him and held him at the listening post for a small wasted fraction of time. If they were prepared to go to this length and rub out an accredited I.G.O. agent, .they must feel sure of their ground. Or the stakes were high enough to accept the risk. One thing was crystal clear: *Interstellar Two Nine* had not met with a regular accident. It was bound up with very much bigger issues.

Then he was through the arch and ploughing through soft pile to range around and check out the transparent walls for an exit to the roof.

When he had it, it was locked and he used his laser to melt out the wards.

Outside there was starlight above an elaborate formal garden with cultivated beds, fountains, a copse of miniature trees and tiled paths for a barefoot walker. Rounding an angle of heavily scented shrubs with waxy, trumpet-shaped flowers, he was faced by a long oval swimming pool with a large white plastic duck paddling in slow circles. On the far side was a low marble pavilion with striped awnings.

It was all very elaborate to be served by one private entrance and he reckoned there could well be another way in for the *hoi polloi* when Scarphe was playing host.

As he reached the end of the building, skirting the pool at a jog trot, the whole set exploded into light. From being a black-and-white job below the threshold for color, it suddenly rioted with every hue on the palette. At the same time the duck, with a

built-in phototropic response, perked up to take-off
speed and began a low flight around the oval.

Fletcher pressed on for sanctuary. Unseen lights
had gone on in the pavilion. Inside there were more
yellow cushions, a wall-to-wall bar with an android
ready to serve drinks, another spiral staircase and the
terminal of an elevator shaft.

Since they believed he was there, the obvious action was to send up a party to flush him out. For
that matter, some strategist might just have decided
to work logically from the top and go down floor by
floor. Either way it was all bad.

They would use a big force. Several trips for this
cage. There was the germ of an idea in that and he
moved off into the rear, where there was the usual
clutter of ancillary rooms, kitchen, showers, changing booths.

He found what he wanted in a storeroom full to
the door with a jumble of spare furniture. There was
a rectangular trap in the roof.

He climbed the swaying pile conscious that time
must be running out, shoved the trap back on its
hinge and hauled himself through. When his eyes
adjusted he found there was enough light welling up
from ventilation grilles to orientate by.

It was all one open space and the elevator trunk
was carried through to the roof as an openwork lat-
tice of metal beams. As he reached it, there was a
rush of stale air and the cage homed on its stops in
the pavilion.

Fletcher squeezed through the frame and dropped
slowly to full-arm stretch. He could hear voices below
and the quick tramp of feet as the detail did a smart
fan-out from the cage. He felt for the roof with his
toes and settled his feet one at a time, taking infinite

care to make no noise. Then he went down to a full knee-bend and steadied himself with his hands.

He was hardly set before the cage began to drop into complete darkness.

When it stopped, its operator barked out an order and the fabric vibrated under another rush. They were wasting no time to get a maximum search party to the top. Unless he wanted to go up and down like a yoyo he had to get off.

He straightened up, felt the wall for the lintel of the next floor stop and heaved himself on to it. Flattened like a bas relief with his back crawling with *angst*, he heard the hatch close and the motor take the load. Draught lifted the hair on the back of his neck and the cage was past. He found the inner release catch and eased open the door a centimeter.

There was one Crotonian guard with his carbine at the ready standing at the break in the spiral staircase, looking up.

Fletcher thumbed the catch on his laser for a wide-angle stunning beam and shot through the gap. The man fell forward, reached a point of balance against the handrail and lost interest.

Fletcher made the stairhead at a run and caught the carbine as it fell.

Carrying on down the spiral stairway he reached ground level without giving himself time to think. There were two Crotonians on the bottom landing, both standing with their backs to a double-leaf outer door. They had been left there as a backstop but he was clearly not expected. One had leaned his carbine against the wall and was rolling himself a long black cigarette. The other was meditatively scratching his crotch and whistling a low air.

The wide-angle beam fixed them in a set piece like shopfitters' dummies and Fletcher moved delicately between them so that no vibration would disturb the balance. The whistler, lips pursed for a soundless O, petrified in midscratch, would have his problems when his sergeant did his rounds.

Outside, he was on the broad terrace that surrounded the tower block, but on the far side from the porch where the shuttles had touched down. There was a six-meter open stretch to a low ornamental wall with crocus-shaped beacons alternatively throwing yellow and blue light.

Fletcher forced himself to walk across slowly. He was the only moving object either way to the corners. At the wall he sat down, swung over his legs, turned around and dropped three meters to a sloping lawn dotted with shrubs and flowerbeds. He stood still to get his bearings and then struck out to meet a surface road that must lead into the area of the terminal.

The air was soft, warm, full of scents reminiscent of tropical gardens on Earth. He could have been taking an after-dinner walk from some tourist haven, except that the star map had an unusual tinge of color and had none of the familiar groupings.

It was wholly incongruous that he should be there, alien and alone. There was no sense of personal danger though he knew intellectually that statistics were against him.

That was strange in itself. Had he gotten to a watershed in his personal journey where he no longer cared either way whether he made out or not? There was a limit to experience. After a point you could say, "Enough."

At surface level, however, he was reacting as though survival were a sufficient purpose. Another shuttle traveling very fast was coming from the direction of the terminal and he dived for the shelter of a bush.

He watched it claw to a stop in front of the admin tower. Another batch of security guards spilled out. Anytime now they were going to find that he had slipped the net and the hunt would be on.

A hundred meters away was the outer ring of a housing development, cottages for the labor force: neat two-story boxes with paths and lawns and a parking lot for small surface buggies to get them to their allotted sector of the coal face.

He went for it at a sprint, threw himself into the nearest car of the line and took in its driving console in a racing, concentrated scan. He was moving off when a high keening wail began to sound out from the tower block.

It was the general alert for industrial disaster and Crotonians shot from their house doors like so many jackrabbits, as though they had been waiting in the hall for it.

There was a stampede for the car park. Fletcher leaned out of his cab pointing towards the terminal. He shouted in speech tones, "Accident. At the port. Get along there," and fed in all the power there was.

In the absence of any other guide, it was taken up in Crotonian as a rallying cry. Motors kicked into life. When he spared a second to look back, he found the field strung out behind him, lights in a blaze. It was as good a camouflage as he could get.

He reached the terminal checkpoint two hundred meters ahead of the pack. He could see the IBS shuttle was still on its pad ready for its return trip. A tender was already crossing the tarmac, taking out passengers.

A guard tumbled out of the left-hand booth, belatedly aiming to heave down a black-and-white banded pole that was pointing up like a warning finger.

Fletcher drove for the narrowing V and felt the jar as the beam slapped down on the transom. But he was through and running along the short side of a triangle to beat the toastrack to the rocket.

He went up the companion two at a time and shoved past a flustered steward at the hatch.

"Take me to the commander and then get these people on board but quick."

"He is too busy. We are ready for take-off."

"Now."

Fletcher's laser appeared in his hand and the man's face grayed in the Crotonian equivalent for pallor.

"This way."

It took under a minute but the terminal building had come to life. Two of Scarphe's security tenders were circling the control tower and no doubt telling all.

Fletcher said, "I am sorry to involve you, commander, but I have to insist on the protection of your ship. I am an I.G.O. officer an official business and I require you to take me to Breseus. You can sort it out from there."

The control cabin was familiar. Except that the crew were not sealed up for deep space, it could have been a variant of a starship. They were his kind of people. All eyes were on the captain. They would go along with anything he said.

Speaking slowly, the Crotonian on the command island said, "I respect the I.G.O. service. Take the spare communications couch. We will, as you say, sort it out in Breseus."

In the same deliberate voice he went on, "Seal hatches. Count down as of now. *IBS-45* to Sylean

Terminal, keep clear. Moving in one minute thirty seconds."

There was a spasm of gobbledygook from the speaker which cut off as he flipped a switch and a familiar trembling ran through the fabric.

On the scanner there was a comic silent sequence as a vermilion flower of intense flame unfolded from the pad and every moving unit beat away for cover.

IBS-45 was all systems go.

VI

Medoc, all there was of power on Bromius, Life President and with ambitions to recycle the political setup into a new-style dynasty, looked around the conference table giving nothing away.

He had the face to do it. A mandarin type with a bland inscrutable oval, he was well ahead of the game. Admittedly he could not read far into the mental labyrinth of the two Scotians, but the rest of the O.G.A. representatives were open books. Dirty books at that.

They had enough knowledge of Bromusian expertise in the e.s.p. field to keep a certain guard. But once they began to talk the difficulties of mental control were too great for any but a fakir and Medoc took a certain ironic pleasure in hearing the spoken word and seeing in his mind's eye a running-picture commentary of what was happening simultaneously behind their frank and candid eyes.

The meeting in his private audience room of the sprawling admin complex could have been an inner-wheel consultation of the Outer Galactic Alliance. All the principal powers and most of the sympathizers were represented: Chrysaor; Scotia; Sabazius; Podargon; Garamas; even Soloon whose metallic ovoid people had least in common with any other culture in the galaxy.

Alban the Soloonian had been the last speaker. He was urging the group to consider their identity of interest and move faster with their project. As he said in a pleasant unisex contralto, "A secret of great importance is sooner or later betrayed. The greater the secret, the more likely it is to be sooner. Even an accident could be enough, as we have seen in the case of the research group which stumbled on some classified information. Caution is one thing, dilatoriness is another. We should aim to open the concessions before the end of the month. Then the first ore consignments could be moving before the end of the year."

Medoc had no formal face to look at. The Soloonian's notional head was located at the narrowing apex of his egg—a system of shadowed microgrooving which altered with the shift of the viewing eye and was all things to all men.

But the brain which was the only biological element in the mass was as vulnerable as any other to the e.s.p. probe. The gloss it was putting out in counterpoint to the spoken text was that Soloon was on the nearest thing to a double-headed penny. Most remote of the O.G.A. planets, they were least likely to suffer from I.G.O. reprisals. Also they were virtually indestructible in their underground warrens of rollways. Metal-hungry they were, because infrangom represented a very superior grade in flesh, but they could manage if they had to. Any success of the enterprise would be pure gain; failure could be covered by reasonable collateral.

No trace of knowledge showed in Medoc's tone as he said, "Alban is right to want an early start. Arrangements from my end are almost complete. Contracts have been submitted to I.G.O. for approval. I think they were doubtful, but they could not go against their avowed policy that trade links should cement the peace. We have already begun to mine beryllium, which is superficially identical with infrangom ore. Have no fear, once the flow starts there will be no difficulty in substituting infrangom for beryllium. Your supplies are assured."

A high-shouldered Sabazian, lumpy as a rock figure, with eye disks of flat black obsidian, said, "Your price is too high."

Medoc read quick agreement in more than one head, followed by a modifying thought that infrangom had no ceiling price when you got right down to it. Any advanced technical society had to have it or fall behind. For spacecraft, there was no substitute at the weight which would put an incombustible lining on the rocket tubes, nothing with the tensile strength for strucural ribs—the list was endless. It was the wonder metal of the age. But scarce. This new supply on Bromius was the first for a century. They were lucky to be in on the ground floor, whatever the old bastard wanted for it. And for that matter, with the O.G.A. fleets back on full strength, a day might come when Medoc would have to do as he was told.

Before Medoc could reply, he had an ally in Gaur, the single Laodamian at the meeting. Hunched apelike over the table, massive choppers in a bony grin, he said, "Some items have no price tag. If you think about it, you will see that Bromius could have kept this to itself. Or gotten a pat on the head from I.G.O. for declaring it. We have an opportunity here to rebuild the fortunes of the Rim planets. Expensive operations will be needed to keep the traffic secret. The price is not too high. Nor is the personal guarantee to President Medoc. We are in such agreement that I believe we can leave the detail to the executives to carry through. I am prepared to sign the undertaking . . . though perhaps before we break up we could have the latest bulletin on the Earth ship which is looking into the loss of that ethnology outfit."

"Certainly." Medoc looked around and read agreement. The Laodamian was a hard one to read so he only had the overt script to follow. But at that level it was all good. The answer was simple enough. He had not taken his good news to I.G.O. because they would have said thank you and taken over the infrangom deposits for the good of the greater number with maybe a plaque for himself in their hall of fame. He was more concerned with his own greater good: power now and status in the world while he was still able to enjoy it. O.G.A. offered that, being advocates of self-help, and of freedom to do your thing whatever the cost to the less enterprising in blood or tears.

Medoc went on: "The starship with the investigator on board has left Croton and is approaching Bromius space. Her commander may have some plan of following the path of the missing ship. If that is so he will not arrive here. On the other hand, if he should request direct access to Tragasid spaceport, he will be accommodated. Thereafter he will be dealt with. You need have no fear on that score. He is following normal channels. It was obvious that an inquiry would be made. He will go away satisfied or he will not go away at all."

Omphal the Sabazian, who had questioned the price, showed that being bloody-minded was a way of life. "I hope we can be assured of that. He was not

107

supposed to get as far as Croton, but he evaded the Scotian. What about that? There has been no explanation given. I thought Scotian interceptor craft were the best in the business."

The Scotians made no comment, staring in front of them with reptilian stillness. Medoc said, "He has been lucky."

"Then we should see that his luck runs out."

Lucky Fletcher was watching the elastic swing of Tamar Kelly's red-gold bell of shining hair and it was distracting him from his midwatch chore of putting a commentary into the log. To save any doubt it was going at some cost to robot receptionists at Northern Hemisphere Space H.Q. and the wandering artificial asteroid that held the admin center of I.G.O. The momentary delay could have been calculated in gold itself.

He cleared his mind of every other consideration and spoke quietly into the battery of microphones. "Entering area of search in four minutes' time. First class cooperation from all hands." That was the least that could be said of a team that had put *Interstellar X* dead center on the last fix for the missing ship. "Action call coming up. Over and out."

Then he noted the time at 1423 hours precisely and stubbed down on the general alarm.

When the controlled chaos subsided and the command cabin was full of spacesuited figures, he found he had every executive report on his console at 1425.29. Granted they had been expecting the action-stations call, but it was still a response that could hardly have been bettered by a crack military unit.

He opened the operational phase with a laconic, "Well done, all."

Many repetitions of Walker's last tape had fixed

the details in his mind, so that the harmonic's of Walker's voice overlaid his own in a mental echo chamber.

When they hit the vector every circumstance was right. *Interstellar X* was lined up solid as a marble bank for a home run.

Now he was completely sure. The figures had suggested it. The total situation confirmed it. Nothing external to the ship had caused deviation at that point. Whatever it was had come from inside. Something or someone had persuaded Walker to change course. And if so, where had he gone?

To that there was only one answer.

Interstellar X had turned as though leaving Bromius space to work over to a line that would end in a proving orbit around Croton. Before putting an answer on record, he felt that he should run through the sequence once more.

"Number one. Speak to Croton. Make a circuit and run back through this alignment."

It was committing all hands to another thirty minutes in their private shells, but he coldly used all his ration of unrecoverable time in going through all the data once more.

When *Interstellar X* ran again into the critical segment of the chart, he knew with absolute finality that he was right. *Two Nine* could only have changed course one way. She had dropped out of the Croton beam, fallen back into the gravisphere of Bromius and spiraled down to an unscheduled and unannounced landfall on that hospitable planet.

Any other course would have been picked up by any one of a dozen tracking stations. Croton, with an accepted plot and everything set for a straightforward run, would not be able to scramble the finely tuned beam and pick her up from scratch on general search. *Two Nine* had disappeared into the screen of a planetary gravisphere where there was enough trash about to conceal her from any probe except one from that planet itself.

That left the onus on Bromius control. They were not space-minded. At least they gave the impression that they only maintained beam facilities out of courtesy to I.G.O. Their report, "No knowledge of this craft," could figure.

Saying that she was down on Bromius was like saying the needle was somewhere in the hay.

Dag Fletcher switched in a blown-up still of the planet on the main scanner. It was largely liquid. Huge areas of shallow sea with chains of low island covered the northern and southern polar regions, leaving a continuous equatorial girdle of fertile land with a climate basically similar to that of the Florida coast. There were millions of square kilometers of ocean, many thousands of small islands.

Only seconds of tolerance remained for a decision. Walker's tape was running on in his head with that tiny unmistakable click of an opening hatch. Walker had gone in from this point. He could follow. The corvette had power to penetrate an atmosphere and move out again without a landfall.

"Stand by. Major course change. Number one. Set it up to home on Bromius. Now it is."

Scullion went in without hesitation, though he had less cause to know what the corvette could do. He whipped his team into what could be suicidal action.

"Home on Bromius. Check. Power one. Retro. Full. Now."

Deceleration was fierce. Before the effect was fully worked out, Scullion had the new course. He reeled off figures for Hobbs to process. Urgent bleeps told that the ship was responding to Bromius gravity and picking up a new acceleration. At the precise microsecond, he called for thrust and she came around under control, dipping her cone to a new target.

"One to commander. Bromius course set."

There was a good hour before anything critical could come up. They might as well have the comfort of taking a spell out of the clumsy gear that no number of missions ever made space crew learn to take without irritation.

"Thank you, number one. Stand down."

Tamar Kelly arrived from her outpost in pale blue pants and a tunic top with a motif of acanthus leaves. It reminded him that there was still a portion of the watch to go.

He unsealed slowly, trying to think ahead. But he could not see beyond the present move. He watched her arrange her dog, leering towards Sinclair's desk. Every new pose it found gave a fresh dimension to depravity. Now it had settled for a kind of sated lechery.

If their luck depended on it, they were likely to find it double-edged.

Speculation cut off as Bromius control, which must have had them in view for some time, put in a gentle request for identification.

It would have been hard to find an official anywhere else in the galaxy, where split-second timing was part of the operating pattern, using such a courteous, old-world formula. Commanders at the end of a long mission had been known to be driven to the point of maniacal fury by it.

Fletcher answered in the same vein. He had found that it actually speeded the sequence to play along their way.

The distant operator began to send a detailed

111

pilotage spiel for a planetfall on Tragasid. It was the updated equivalent of taking the pilot on board.

On the internal net, he alerted Tamar Kelly to work out her own landing plot on the data. Courtesy was one thing, but he wanted a collateral.

She had it done in a commandable rush of deft precise movement which was a pleasure to watch in its own right, as Sinclair came in and settled himself at the power desk. If differed from the Bromius figure by enough to send *Interstellar X* on a splashdown, two hundred kilometers from the nearest neck of land at a speed that would dig her grave in the sea bed.

Fletcher looked at the two sets of data. It would have been easier if they had come from Randle Hobbs though he was nowhere near as good a mathematician. He would have accepted them without question. Coming from the spectacular Kelly he had to be sure he was not being influenced by nonprofessional angles.

The hesitation was small enough, but it was noticed. Tamar Kelly's brown eyes were enigmatic in a straight stare that made an almost visible beam path, from her console to the central figure on the command island.

In fact she was seeing the problem from inside his head in an act of empathy which she had not experienced before with any other person. She was all ready to say, "Hold fast on that. I'll work the data again for confirmation," when he got in first.

Dag Fletcher had cut corners on all complications. There was only one issue. You either trusted your crew or you did not, and if you did you put your life on it. "Pass your version into navigation, Tamar. Sort it out with Bromius control when we get down."

Critical for a lover, Dave Sinclair said in a carrying whisper, "Holy cow, Ginger, you'd better be right. If not, God grant me two seconds only to twist the head off of that canine contortionist. I only hope you know what you're doing."

When the crew were reassembled and *Interstellar X* was dropping out of the sky with Tragasid spaceport dead center on the scanner, the decision was vindicated.

Fletcher had time to weigh a simple theory. Maybe there was no real mystery at that. It could be that he was being oversubtle. If Bromius control had made an error, *Two Nine* could have foundered with all hands. Its dubious mission was irrelevant. With all their charm the Bromusians were total realists. Nothing could reawaken the dead, so why go through the face-losing rigmarole of an inquiry? The decision to land on Bromius had been taken unexpectedly. They were bombproof if they stuck to their story of nothing seen.

For some seconds, he felt he had it clear. But intuition would not be bucked. There was too much involved to be settled on one mathematical error.

A gentle Bromusian voice was going on in his left ear about the final phases of planetfall. He stopped thinking and went into the familiar action of landing the corvette.

It was still a pleasure. Years of careful precision in freight and passenger ships of the line gave way to the panache that was possible in a military craft with this power-to-weight ratio. Even Holdbrook was beginning to fidget before he called, "Power. Retro. Now," and steadied the falling silver pencil above its designated pad.

He took her down in a dive that settled her to within half a meter of the full telescoping depth of

113

her jacks. Then as she rose slowly to full commanding height he was saying on the closed circuit, "Commander to all hands. On no account is the ship to be vacated. At all times an operational detail must remain on watch. I shall be going ashore on a procedural visit. Power two and communications two with me in the scout car. Ceremonial rig. Number one, remember you have power to devastate Tragasid. Do not accept an order to leave the ship even if it comes from me. If in doubt speak to I.G.O. military command."

Scullion said, "Copilot to commander, check," and left the air vacant again.

Wreaths of gray coolant floated past the direct observation ports, shutting out Bromius, giving them a last tenuous isolation from the new environment.

When it cleared the complex of terminal buildings was less than a kilometer off in mellow sunlight and something like a cortege appeared to be setting out. It was all wheeled transport, low open cars loaded with flowers. The situation was slipping into unreality; it would be like looking for a murderer in a friendly kindergarten.

Sinclair had gone to work before the procession was halfway over. The scout car circled the ship once with its I.G.O. pennant straining away stiff as metal and hovered at the main hatch for Tamar Kelly to join the pilot and Fletcher to climb into the rear squab.

Its canopy was back and the Bromusian welcome squad halted to watch. They could see the white uniformed figure of a dark powerful subaltern at the controls; beside him a vivid red-gold head and the top section of a green-and-gold stiff tabard; in the rear, a tall angular figure, hair weathered to a uni-

114

form pale ash—when the car bore down on the column, gray-green and noncommittal.

Sinclair ran level with the leading car which contained the port superintendent and two brilliantly dark hostesses in rose madder saris. Following the custom of the place these draped the right shoulder and bared the left side to the thigh, where they kept station by short loops of narrow silver chain.

It sounded harsh and incongruous in his own ears, but Fletcher went into the formal opening gambit which he had used too often for memory. "Commander Fletcher of the I.G.O. service. Earth ship *Interstellar X* European Space Corporation."

He might have saved his breath. Gentle lilting voices, making Earth language into an exotic dialect, went into elaborate welcome. *Leis* were handed over by delicate, fine-boned hands. The total impression was that the Bromusians had waited all their lives to this point for the rare pleasure of welcoming these three strangers.

Fletcher felt undermined like a sandheap in a warm tide. It would be churlish to stand out against it. He picked up some of the tone. Sinclair had a bludgeoned look as though beaten by a scented cosh, but Tamar Kelly was sitting still, fighting a rearguard. Her eye when she looked his way held something like disbelief. No doubt she was feeling overdressed and at a disadvantage.

It would be interesting to see how she made out. Physically there could be no greater difference in type. Then he noticed two limp black paws over the rim of the equipment tray. She was taking no chances; she had brought her lucky dog.

Ritual welcome or not, Fletcher vetoed any further move towards the ship. To soften the direct negative, he transferred to the leading car and reconciled himself to the role of sacrificial lamb.

It was not too rough: perfume with a harmonic of sandalwood, pale ivory, petal-soft skin, a bare hemisphere breast nudging pneumatically against his right arm.

The girl read his interest before the catalogue had fully formed in his head and crowded closer in a kind of total willingness to oblige.

She said, "Lida, commander, if it pleases you."

Tamar Kelly turned round from the front seat, reacting to the very sexy harmonic and gave him a considering look as if he were now revealed as the nympholept of all time.

To make it clear that his motives at least were pure, he pushed out the first banal question that formed in his mind.

"Have you been attached to the space service for long?"

"I have had the pleasure of welcoming visitors to our planet for six months."

That would cover the period of *Two Nine*'s loss. "You speak the Earth language very well. Have you met many Earth starships?"

It was too raw. The brown eyes were laughing at him. She had gotten around to the point before he had framed it in words. She scrubbed around it. "Thank you. You are kind to compliment me. We on Bromius find it easy to learn languages. We are able to go right to the heart of communication and understand the patterns from the inside. Thirza, my companion, requires only four days to become fluent in a new language."

The linguist herself said nothing. She had twined a supple leg around Fletcher's left calf and was putting on a gentle squeeze. It could well be that, like many another, she knew many tongues and had nothing to say in any one of them. But on the direct action front she was an instant communicator.

At the terminal there was VIP treatment. Without physically unrolling a red carpet, they projected the idea that there was one there. Every routine procedure was smooth and taken with courteous apology. There was a brief stop in a blue and white anteroom for a quarantine check where a young doctor fussed around Tamar Kelly in frank delight, doing a good rehabilitation job for her ego.

She was outside experience. The ancient people of Bromius had long passed the era of differing racial types. They were now all very similar, men standard height at one and a half meters, women fractionally less, uniformly black-haired, brown-eyed, lightly and delicately built. Except for the very rare case. Like Hulda, who must have been classed as an albino deviant and made to feel a stranger on her own planet. Tamar's spectacular coloring and athletic figure got a rare press.

That and the dog. She carried him drooping his unseemly head on his paws over her arm.

The doctor, shifting his admiring eye from her hair to see what she was carrying with the polite aim of offering to be a help, leaped back half a meter, where he was brought up by his office wall.

Flight thwarted, he spoke up for science: "What is that?"

"It's my lucky dog."

"Lucky dog?"

"A kind of mascot. A charm."

"It is not very charming, that one. What is it called?"

"It has no name. Once you name a thing you give limits to it. Put it in a kind of box."

117

"That is a very interesting observation. But a box would be no bad thing. A lead-lined casket would not be too much."

For Bromius that was plain speaking. Fletcher reckoned it was time to move into the conversation. "Do you have many Earth visitors through your unit?"

Shaken he might be, but the medico had enough social poise for a civil answer. "Not as many as we would like, of course. Feel free to consult the record. You might be gratified to see the name of some old acquaintance."

It was pat enough to mean that he had been briefed to say just that. There would be no point in looking.

Half an hour later they were free, with a reduced train of equerries, to press on along a broad tree-lined avenue that went straight over undulating open country for the metropolis of Tregasid. There was one massive white limousine with a plexiglass dome, two outriders on scooters and Sinclair, to his great disgust, tagging on alone in the scout car.

Tregasid was set on a low plateau, surrounded by gently rising hills. Four metropolitan through-ways homed on its central, oval piazza and divided the city into mathematically equal quadrants. Concentric interzonal connectors, tree-lined and spacious, were spaced out like ripples in a colored pool with the last one making a ring road around the city and giving it a clear-edged definition.

Private traffic was excluded from the seven inner rings with all necessary services restricted to the two hours before dawn. The outriders were now seen to be more than ornamental. Sirens hitting a melodious wail, they had to clear a swath through pedestrians who seemed to look on the roadways as an extension of hearth and home.

The single striking impression was of silence. Anywhere else such a mass of moving people would be giving off a racket like a busy jungle. But here there was a hiss like surf on a quiet beach.

They moved aside to let the convoy through and closed up again behind it in a moving tide of delicate color. They were an elegant, urbane people, at home in their elegant city. A golden world come again, incapable of guile, needing, if anything, protection from the harsh realities of power politics in an ear where they were vulnerable to attack from warmongers outside their gravisphere.

Mosaics in blue and gold, fountains and trees with broad yellow leaves, and low walls, decorated with a continuous freize of gazelles and lotus flowers, floored the central piazza.

They drew up under the long apricot awning of the State Guest Hotel and Dave Sinclair, bemused and heavily garlanded, brought the scout car alongside and climbed out.

Tamar Kelly followed the direction of his eye, locked on a passing Bromusian girl who had slipped off her sari for greater comfort and was carrying it over her left arm. Kelly said with feeling, "It's a minor miracle you got here. If you would be so good as to take that lecherous simper off of your face, I'd be obliged for you to dig my overnight bag out of the freight bay. Dear God. They've got me doing it now. It's like a disease."

She lifted her dog and draped it over the entry port rim. The minute vibrations of the car's powerpack gave a kind of life to its mobile bloodshot eyes. A commissionaire, nipping smartly from the lobby to do his thing on welcome, tripped over his feet and was saved by Sinclair whose reaction time though dulled was still good. As he set the man on his feet a backup party of three smiling girls in fine transparent linen tunics with narrow gold belts appeared, walking slowly, hands held out palms uppermost.

All in all, Fletcher felt that he was being submerged in a pink cloud of unknowing. Their suite when they were allowed to reach it underlined the illusion. It was a pastel-shaded womb flooded with the rose-madder-tinged sunlight peculiar to Bromius.

A wide verandah overlooking a central courtyard connected the three principal rooms. Floor-to-ceiling windows on that side had the local variant of a venetian blind, thousands of small translucent leaves pivoted at the touch of a lever.

Tamar Kelly's room was lavishly equipped with every cosmetic device that any woman traveler from any corner of the galaxy had ever asked for and some were bizarre.

Its total effect brought out a latent fighter for women's rights. She stood her lucky dog amongst the paraphernalia of the oldest art with one rear leg realistically cocked and reckoned that he cut it all down to size.

Bromusian clothing was laid out for approval. But she decided to stick with her tabard. No prude about her own figure, she felt that there was enough nudity about.

The bed was a huge circle, solid to the floor, with half a meter of cunning upholstery. An archway screened by hanging lines of gold and silver leaves led to a sunken scallop-shell tub, heavily scented with exaltolides. Fighting a rearguard she said, "Yuk," and went out to the verandah for what fresh air might be moving about.

She was still standing by the baluster watching the few people currently using the garden area when Fletcher and Sinclair appeared from their pads. More tactful or suggestible, whichever way you looked at it, they had changed into fine linen tunics and narrow white pants.

Sinclair said, "When in Rome. What's all this, Tamar? Why aren't you showing your pubic spirit?"

Sorting out which of two cutting replies to make, she was thwarted altogether by a girl in harem pants and a navel jewel who seemed to materialize out of the woodwork with a silver tray carrying a folded green paper.

The message was for Fletcher but the girl bowed ceremonially to all hands.

Medoc was wasting no time. It was an invitation which could class as a summons to present themselves at Dusk 1, in the presidential lodge no less. Handwritten by the headman himself, it included a hope that all pleasure would attend their stay.

Tamar said, "Dusk 1?"

"Domestically we still use the old system. Sometimes it is confusing for visitors. Daytime hours are counted from dawn—one to ten. The hours of darkness from sunset—one to ten again. You will find a conversion table in your room."

"I think I can work it out."

"Since all the inhabited land is on the equator and day and night are always of equal length, it is more convenient here than it would be elsewhere."

"I can see that."

"It was a pleasure to be able to explain it to you."

"I am glad you are glad."

She backed away, followed to the last by Sinclair's admiring eye. Tamar Kelly turned on her heel and withdrew to her scented burrow, a minority of one in the euphoria.

For one so keen to see them, Medoc was taking the last step slowly. When they were ushered into the presidential drawing room it appeared to be empty, like opening a blown egg.

It was a curious room, having no precise shape or boundaries, with trick optical effects and archways opening off into vistas that the eye could not plumb. Any agoraphobiac would have blown his mind. Concentration was a real difficulty.

A focus was suddenly provided by a Bromusian girl who appeared as though by sleight of hand from nowhere in particular. She could have stood in for the symbol of the ethnic type: slim to the point of fragility, oval face of exact classical proportion, dark hair interwoven with electrum thread, wearing a notional seethrough caftan that was no more than a fluid overlay of pale apricot shifting light.

Sinclair, weakened by exposure, stood with his mouth open. Tamar Kelly, reckoning he would drool any minute now, turned her back and put in some close study on a large decorated amphora as though another one might be expected to whip out of it. It was left to Fletcher to take the extended hands and listen to a bell-like voice say, "I am Alva. My father will be along. Sit down and tell me all about your starship."

It was all a non-event that matched the vague formlessness of the place. Medoc, when he arrived, seemed to have no defined purpose. He turned the conversation away from the aim of the starship's visit. They drank straw-colored wine from pale green goblets, ate some small scented cakes. Tamar Kelly looked at the decor. Sinclair watched Alva as though hypnotized. Fletcher did his best to get to the hard questions and had the impression that he was adrift in a sea of cotton wool.

On the way back after a long silence Tamar Kelly said positively, "It just isn't true. I simply don't believe it."

Sinclair had not surfaced from his private fantasy. Fletcher had come to the conclusion that the visit had been a pretext for Medoc to weigh them in his own balance and maybe use some sophisticated gear to check what they had in their minds.

He suddenly recognized that she had been neglected and leaned forward to face her across the zombie.

Her brown eyes were very serious. "What's that then? What don't you believe?"

"Nobody can be that perfect. She's a phony."

"Who is this?"

"Alva. Every living one of them for that matter. They're too good to be true."

"You're not the first to say that."

"So you agree with me?"

"I keep an open mind."

In the soft glow of the roof light, her hair was moving like liquid gold as she spoke. It triggered off a line of pillow talk that surprised him when it was out and about.

"Be generous. There is no one on this planet with hair as beautiful as yours. They have to have some virtues to make up."

"You're falling into their ridiculous jargon."

"No, truly."

Ten minutes after arrival she was on the verandah and tapping at the glass of his door.

When he operated the leaf screen he saw that she had changed to Bromusian rig, a transparent turquoise *ao dai* with a fine electrum chain slanting across her trim abdomen.

But it was a complaint to the ship's captain. When he opened the hatch she said, "I knew they were phony."

"Tell me all."

"My dog's gone. Some Bromusian creep has shanghaied my lucky dog."

It would be good news to some, but he was spared any opinion. The video on his wall console gave a discreet ping and glowed into life.

The receptionist tuned in a neat pose as though leaning into the room for a confidential whisper said, "There is a call for you from your starship, commander."

He said, "Hold on. I'd better take that."

Scullion's face replaced the operator. "The chairman's been through, commander. Wants you to call back. He has a message to pass on."

"Fine. I'll use the scout car. See you in fifteen minutes."

Tamar Kelly had gone, her good line spoiled by competition. It was not until he was lifting the car off its skids that he realized she could have told him about the dog without changing into a seethrough shift.

VII

Scullion said, "I didn't want to go into detail on an open link. Your query to Frazer's been answered. We're holding the first relays open, so it shouldn't take long for a hookup."

Hobbs did it in under five minutes and Spenser was rasping into the control cabin as though from across the pad.

Scrambled at European Space and unscrambled by a subtle transducer on *Interstellar X*, his words crossed the unimaginable distance in a private company code. He said, "I must be a fool to send you on that sort of mission. I ought to know better. It stood out a sea league that there was more to it than a straight-up accident. What have you been hatching with Frazer?"

"I asked him a question."

"That's no good answer. In fact it's a lousy answer. He's still working on it, but you've worried him. The nearest squadron is out beyond Neleus. It will take time to move up. Meanwhile you have the only armed I.G.O. ship in the area. You have to stay there until he gives the word. If that's what you wanted you've got it; but I don't like it one small bit. I expect a top executive of this company to have its interests at heart. I'll leave it to you to work out the cost when you get back. And you can find some way to offset it against economies. The company isn't a government. It can't stand this kind of loss."

"If this isn't sorted out, there might not be a company."

"You say. You say."

"There's something else you can pass on to Frazer. Tell him that the Sylea Industrial Complex on Croton has been entertaining an oversize Scotian delegation and that the director tried to have me killed. I think that *Two Nine* got involved in something, possibly by accident. I'll report as and when I can. Since we have a military role, you can charge that to I.G.O."

He spent half an hour in the ship checking it for military readiness and carefully aligned the main armament for a selective blast on the admin center of Tregasid. When it was done he locked the firing stud and handed Scullion the key. "For God's sake don't let that out of your hand. I can't see it being needed, but if it is you have a bargaining lever that should make Medoc think twice."

As he was ready to leave a red glow from the port observation window moved them both to look out across the apron. A new arrival, hidden by the glare of her own retro, was dropping to a pad half a kilometer off.

Fletcher said, "You could put somebody on a survey of what ships are in port. Watch for personnel movements. List them by type, nationality, purpose in being here at all. Most of it should be on the shipping movement board at the terminal, but direct observation will confirm it. OK?"

"OK. We'll watch this end. Don't worry about your back."

On the return trip, Fletcher lifted the scout car to its ceiling and took a bat's-eye view of Tregasid. At night the city shimmered like a huge jewel. Ground beacons running out on main compass points to orientate the airborne traveler were bright rays from its perimeter.

In the distance, smaller invisible cities showed up as a pale nimbus on the horizon. It was a considerable ornament of time and a high marker for human culture.

Crossing over an Earth city he would have felt kinship with the unseen people who had devised it as their living machine and some share in human pride at the achievement. But here he was an alien. Basically he was involved in a dream sequence where no real communication was possible.

Even Hulda had come and gone as a dream. Maybe he was no longer remembering that sequence as it

126

happened. It had all been illusion with no true communication passed either way.

He sensed that there was a craft overhead before he saw it on the scout car's small scanner. Automatically he looked left for a clear way to sideslip down. But there was another moving in, blocking the path. Cars had moved in, boxing him from every quarter with another slipping ahead to plug the last hole.

Before he could blame himself for lack of concentration, search beams from every craft swung and centered so that the small car was floodlit from stem to stern. The international call panel on his console went into spasm.

That at least was good. They wanted to talk. He flipped to receive and an incongruously gentle and musical voice spoke out of the woodwork. "City Air Police, commander. I am sure you are unaware that you are breaking traffic regulations. No flight is permitted over the city after Dusk 4. I must request you to follow the lead car, which will escort you to your hotel."

That was efficient—a very neat operation. He was annoyed that he had left himself wide open for it.

All the cars except the one in front and the one immediately above sheered away and were gone. They had shown how easily they could do it and seemed to say that even a barbarian would understand the language of power.

For a moment he was tempted to evade the guide car, but there was no point. Time enough to buck the system if he had to.

A voice from the console confirmed it. "That is a wise decision, commander. Good night."

The shadow of the car above slid away from over his dome and he felt a tension go out of the air which was out of all proportion to the simple act.

The organizing genius must have been aboard that one and his mind-reading gear was on a short-range beam. Probably not effective at more than six or seven meters, but enough to deflate the ego. If you had no privacy in your head, where could it be found?

He was still pondering that one as he left the scout car at the porch and made his way through the hotel to his suite. Not every Bromusian had the gift or he would have made no friends on his passage. He remembered Hulda had spoken briefly about it as a guild secret. Certain Alpha citizens only were allowed to develop the e.s.p. craft. All Bromusians had a natural flair for it, but the real experts were specially chosen and trained, becoming what amounted to members of an inner circle.

In his room he paced about, trying to think it through. Then he recognized that he could be virtually in an experimental pen. If they could do it in the air without special preparation they could certainly line up a sitting target. A digest of his every thought could be going on record. It would be safest to stick to erotic fantasy.

Free association at that point switched in a still of Tamar Kelly in her electrum chain. He should warn her to keep her mind on insignificant issues. And Sinclair for that matter.

He went to find Sinclair first, tapping on the verandah door and then opening it when there was no answer.

The room was empty. Maybe he had joined the girl anyway. Well, that was their own business. It had nothing to do with him. But he could not avoid an illogical sense of loss and exclusion.

Outside his own door he stopped telling himself

that his warning could wait until morning. Whatever they were thinking would only have significance at a social level. Then he found he had walked on and was hesitating outside her window.

The leafy screen was closed. He turned away, changed his mind and tapped twice on the glass. There was no answer.

The catch was off when he tried the handle and he pushed the door open telling himself he was no more than a voyeur.

Sandalwood perfume drifted through the gap. There was a small courtesy light putting out a dim glow from a ceiling port. Tamar Kelly was lying at five to twelve on top of her circular bed, hair in a dark fan on a pale yellow pillow.

She was alone, asleep and totally vulnerable.

She was so still that he thought suddenly she could be dead. Sinclair taken for questioning and the girl slipping a terminal drug in her toothpaste . . .

Moving silently on thick pile, he reached nine o'clock and leaned over. At this distance, there was visible movement, a regular rise and fall that needed no mine detector to say she was alive.

Her face was very symmetrical and satisfying in sleep, eyelashes in even arcs, forehead smooth and untroubled. It was a mistake to have brought her. Tomorrow, he would get her back to the ship where she would be safe.

The thought was barely formed in his head when the figure had turned into a person with a point of view and an opinion about her own future. Brown eyes, opened wide, filled with alarm which cleared as quickly as she said, "Commander. What is it then?"

At the same time she sat up, proving beyond reasonable doubt that although a still figure had its merit, beauty lay in the curve in motion.

She went on, "Don't worry about me. I've read the small print. There isn't a safe place on a starship in alien space."

"Why do you say that?"

"I thought I heard you say you wanted me back on the ship for safety's sake."

"I thought it, but I didn't say it. This whole suite must be beamed for e.s.p. That was a little feed-back across the channels. Where's Sinclair?"

"I'm not his keeper. There was a call some time ago. An hour maybe. That Alva. Wanted him to join her in some clambake."

"Just Sinclair?"

"I could have gone, but the way it was worded I didn't want any part of it. I don't fancy playing gooseberry. Mind you, I did wonder whether he didn't need an escort. She has him in thrall."

"Do you mind that?"

"Dave's all right, but it doesn't break my heart, if that's what you mean."

There was a lull in the conversation and an awkwardness that could only be broken one way. He could move closer or farther off.

A puritanical conscience triggered off the thought that he was strictly uninvited and was taking unfair advantage as the officer in command of the mission. It was enough to move him away by a few centimeters, a token withdrawal which was nevertheless understood.

She stretched out a long arm for a wrap on a *pouffe*, breasts moving like lithe pale fish in a silk net.

"What was it, commander? You didn't come in to ask about the uneven tenor of my love life."

"True. It was the security angle. Amber sequence for all personnel ashore."

It would be hard to practice thought control for twenty-four hours out of twenty-four, but it would at least make e.s.p. less profitable.

"That's easy. I don't know what it's all about anyway."

Fletcher had gotten himself to the door. "I'm sorry I disturbed you. With Sinclair gone I had to check that you were all right. Then you were so still I thought you were dead."

"And now you know I'm not."

It was all surface chat to stop thought. He could not think of a good exit line so he said, "See you then," and left.

Tamar Kelly wandered over to her dressing table and looked at herself soberly in the glass. She pushed a piano key with a pictograph of a harp and Bromusian music flooded the set from hidden speakers. Very sugary, hitting the common denominator of every nostalgic tune that had ever been devised—strings climbing in unison to a climax that was never reached, bass striding down into brown depths.

After five minutes of it she had heard enough and went slowly back to bed, doing like the man said, thinking of nothing in particular. The handiest focus for noncontroversial thought was Fletcher himself. She speculated about the radiation burn that gave his left eyebrow an interesting twist and wondered if the station gossip were right about the Bromusian Commissar.

Stretched out again on her large bed designed impurely for company, she switched off like a good sailor and drifted into sleep.

A patient Laodamian watched the rhythms on an

oscillograph fall into the pattern for a sleeping subject and transferred her cell to a pending unit.

Fletcher was half an hour before he went for the sack. The other Earthman was still on the town. There was nothing more to do. So far, except for the fact that the commander knew or suspected that he was being watched, there was nothing to report. Still, he was not paid by results. It was all one to him; another hour and his relief would come and he could work in a little fantasy for himself.

Fletcher went on foot to the I.G.O. consulate in Tregasid. It was half a kilometer off on the second interzonal connector from the central piazza. He took Tamar Kelly along out of simple compassion. Sinclair, hardly speaking over the communal breakfast on the terrace, was poor company for a faithful dog. He answered yes or no and then relapsed into a closed-circuit memory link like a pig gorged on cream. Whatever Alva had done with him, she had given him some pictures for his album.

Tamar's expressive eyes made Fletcher a present of her opinion and she was ready in thirty seconds flat when he asked if she wanted to join him.

At street level, among the people, menace was a nonstarter. Mild sunlight and a temperature rock steady at twenty Celsius showed Tregasid at its best.

It was a civilized city, dedicated to the comfort of its citizens. They could have strayed onto the set for an expensive musical thronged with delicate characters in costume. Any time a hidden orchestra might strike up and the whole company swing into line for an opening chorus.

Tamar Kelly had gone back to her ceremonial tabard. Fletcher was in uniform. Both were taller and heavier than the Bromusians in the street. There was a growing sense of fantasy, a dream world. They were the only living people in a court of shadows.

Tamar Kelly's voice sounded loud in her own ears as she said, "It could only be an accident. If this lot are involved at all, it's an accident. I can see them covering up almost out of politeness or just to avoid a scene, but that's about as far as they'd go. They wouldn't plot to take a dime out of a piggy bank. I never saw such a peaceful, nonviolent lot."

They had passed into a short tree-lined connecting way between two zonal rings with a floor of black basalt polished like glass. Foliage mirrored in depth gave the impression that they were suspended over a shimmering yellow pond.

Listening to her agreeable husky voice, Fletcher had gone three paces before the message that his data acquisition network was receiving got any response from decision-making areas in his head. When it registered, his reaction time could be measured in split seconds and the girl reckoned her word had triggered off a small local hurricane.

There was a percussive crack overhead. Fletcher grabbed for her and threw them both flat towards the bole of the nearest tree and the avenue seemed to fill with yellow leaves and small branches.

It was as though the floor had suddenly opened and dropped her into the reflection, except that it was rock hard against her back and Fletcher's stiff-brimmed hat was wedged between them and trying to grind into her sternum.

Through the contact she could feel the thud of falling items through his body arched over her.

It was finished before she could say a word. When she cleared a large spray of palmate leaves from her face, his head was only centimeters away.

For a count of three there was stability. Time for

Fletcher to see that her eyes were not uniformly brown but had small lighter golden chips in the texture and that, although surprised, she was still batting.

His head dropped the last few centimeters of distance, moved by a logic outside reason and he found her mouth, cool, half-open, textured like smooth glass, as unlikely an object as could be found at the bottom of a leaf-filled well. Then he was rolling clear with a laser in his hand looking for a target.

There was none. A circle of Bromusians stepped back a half-pace as he rose from the undergrowth. A massive thigh-thick branch had dropped neatly across the walkway at the point where the next regular step would have taken them.

The Bromusians looked pleased to see him rise from the rubble and one of them began a slow clap. When Tamar Kelly rose head and shoulders out of her bower, it was taken up as a method and the whole circle went into a slow handclap.

Fletcher ignored them. He worked along to the main tree trunk and hauled himself into its branches. The clapping stopped and every eye tracked him on his mission. For their money he could be continuing the morning vaudeville by a death-defying leap from the top and they wanted to miss no part of it.

His assistant picking leaves out of her hair stood at the bottom also looking up. She said, "Shall I pass round your hat? I reckon we'd make a fortune."

Fletcher had found what he was looking for. Given the memory of the quiver of leaves and the glint of bright metal he had seen in the reflection, it was no surprise. The wood had been sheared through at a nicely calculated slant to drop the branch across the avenue.

That was very quick organization, and it pointed

to the e.s.p. link again. Somebody had read the intention of going to the I.G.O. Consulate and the woodman had been briefed at short notice. Maybe other possible routes had been covered in different ways.

He dropped down, retrieved his hat and took her arm. The slow clap started up again and was still sounding its polite congratulation as they reached the end of the avenue.

Tamar Kelly said, "I suppose they mean that. But you could see it another way. It was almost disappointment that there was no pool of blood. A quicker rhythm would be more fitting."

"It's hard to know what these gribbles think. One thing's for sure: just because they look like refined versions of a human being Earth variety, you can't assume they are."

"You should know, by all account."

It was an opening to talk about Hulda, but the time was not right. He let it go and took another tack. "You see what this means? The e.s.p. net at the hotel could only be a government-sponsored operation. So in spite of appearances Medoc knows more than he is admitting. Also he has an interest in blocking the inquiry on *Two Nine*. That ties him in with Scarphe on Croton and with the Scotian interest."

If she was disappointed at the change in topic, she didn't say so. For a dozen steps they went on in companionable silence. He could feel the movement of her hip against his forearm. Earth tissue. Narrowing it down, English tissue. Two of a kind. Lasting communication, if it were to be found anywhere, would be found with a person from your own village.

She said, "They'll try again. Maybe we should all move back to the ship. You can make all the inquiries you want from there."

"True. It might come to that. I'd like to give Medoc a little time to show his hand. We'll stay put for a couple of days."

The I.G.O. commissar, when they found him, was inclined to be critical. He was a Garamasian, round-headed with high shoulders and flat black eye disks that gave nothing away.

Knowing the careful screening that went into selection for the service, Fletcher was prepared to accept that the man was on the right side in the power equation, but his angle was all against complicating the I.G.O. position on Bromius.

"You men of action, commander, are an embarrassment to patient diplomats. It has taken many years to gain acceptance of the I.G.O. point of view on this planet. I do not want to appear to be supporting you against the legitimate government. I see your problem and of course you must investigate the loss of your ship; but, if you will forgive me for saying this, what is one starship against the peace of a whole planet? Small incidents have triggered off catastrophes before this. We are not so secure here that we can afford to alienate the elected government. Think about that and put your interest in the right perspective."

"Do you have a theory?"

"Only that these people set much store on keeping face. It could be that some error on their part contributed to the loss of the ship. Since it has totally disappeared they would see no point in publicizing the detail. The other matters have only a coincidental reference. You have strayed over on to some private commercial deal which the parties concerned want to keep at a confidential level. That is not unusual. Your own company would not advertise its negotiations if it was opening a new freight route. Competitors would be quick to take advantage."

"It is unusual to go to such lengths."

"You say that you and your charming companion were almost killed on the way here. But you were not killed. You are here. This is an ordinary police matter which the Tregasid security force will investigate. There are xenophobes in every country. A group of fanatics are trying to scare you away."

Fletcher gave it up. To some extent the man had a point. It was not good politics to involve the I.G.O. office in a direct confrontation with Medoc. With the peace-keeping force thin on the ground, the balance of power was held largely by bluff.

As he left he said, "It could be that Admiral Frazer will use your diplomatic link to get a message to me. If he does I'd like it right away."

"Of course, commander. I will help in any way I can."

At the Earth consulate, Fletcher tried another tack. It was a small office in the business quarter and the interests of Earth planet were a part-time chore supervised by the manager of a cultural import house.

Every level surface was littered with polished stainless steel cylinders supported on a square plinth by two angled collars of the same diameter.

The consul, a slim graying type with a toothbrush moustache, wide pale forehead, dark expressive eyes, and a spotted bowtie, moved one from a chair for Tamar Kelly and gave it to her when she sat down because there was nowhere else to put it.

That left his hands free to offer one limply to his principal visitor and say, "O'Toole's the name, commander. What can we do for you? If anybody with such a gorgeous friend needs anything more from life."

Held against a living model it was suddenly apparent that the *objets d'art* were no less than highly simplified versions of the female torso and the small room seemed to fill overpoweringly with the evocations of flesh.

Whatever his qualifications as a consul, O'Toole was no slouch at picking up reactions. Watching Fletcher's eye he said admiringly, "Clever. You see what they are, commander. Very popular here. We can't get enough. Copies of course. Brancusi. The quintessential female thing. It transcends cultural boundaries. Representational figures would be Earth-based or Croton-based or what have you; but these go anywhere stripped of local concepts and carry the universal message."

Fletcher said, "No doubt you have the truth of it. But I have a problem which you might throw some light on."

"Everybody has a problem."

O'Toole skipped nimbly behind his desk to transform himself into an official ear and peered out from a staggered array of simplified torsos.

"Do you know Dr. Izod the ethnologist?"

"In which capacity?"

"His or yours?"

"Mine, commander. Mine. As an art factor or a consular official?"

"Either or both."

"Oh. Well. We have handled some material. I'll be frank with you because I like your friend's face."

Tamar Kelly, feeling sensitive as the only prototype of the symbols all around, said, "Thank you."

"Not at all. Not at all. You have a beautiful face. Where was I?"

Fletcher said, "You were going to be frank."

"That's so. You see there are always regulations about moving artifacts of historical importance. Dr. Izod asked for my help to export a few items which were important for his collection. Some figurines as I recall. He could not have done it through official channels. But I included them in a shipment to Croton. Nothing very valuable, but I could see his point of view. A charming man."

"You know he has disappeared?"

"Yes, I know that. I did not see him on this last venture. Very unfortunate. He had an interesting theory about Bromius having originally colonized Croton. Difficult to prove. As far as we know there was no history of space travel here before the space-faring cultures found their way to the planet."

"Has there been any recent increase in trade between Croton and Bromius?"

"Now I wouldn't know that, would I, commander? You could find that in the Institute of Commerce archives. There is pretty constant traffic between the two. They are close. There could be something to Izod's theory. At the time of Izod's last visit, there was a Crotonian group looking into the power generation setup they have here. Very subtle that."

"Where did they go?"

"Close to where Izod was working, as a matter of fact. You know there are islands all over the northern ocean? Very pretty, some. Done up as summer homes for the top brass. Izod was on one of the big ones, where there's a surviving group of primitives. Fairly close, there's one of the shallow enclosed sea areas that they use for power. Something to do with the thermodielectric effect of freezing and thawing a dilute aqueous salt solution. In that latitude the sea freezes at night and thaws by day. Which is very convenient, you must agree. Known I believe as the Ribeiro Process. Very cheap natural power. The Crotonians were hoping the system could be adapted for use on their planet."

"You are very well informed for an art man."

O'Toole waved a deprecating hand which was stopped short of its full flowing gesture by one of the Barncusi torsos. The contact seemed to stir a cord of memory. "I had it all from a very lush doll in the good doctor's entourage."

"Reina Vair?"

"The same. One for folly if ever was. Brought her own etchings in a sling purse."

"She's lost with the ship."

"A loss to mankind."

There was not likely to be anything else. O'Toole was running his fingertips along the polished cylinder in a research for time past, dark eyes full of melancholy.

Fletcher said, "Thanks for the help. One last thing. Do you have a long-distance shuttle I could borrow for a few days?"

"We have some company cars. There could be one we might spare."

"Don't worry about the cost. European Space will pick up the tab."

"Oh. Well, that's different. Certainly. When would you like it?"

"Fourteen hundred. Also mark up the chart for a route to Izod's island. Take it to the first parking lot on the northern metropolitan throughway and leave it for me to pick up. I'll return it there when I'm through."

"Surely. You have a deal."

Tamar Kelly stood up and handed her female torso over the counter. Stuck with it, he was unable to make a farewell gesture and had to pack all possible meaning into a straight look.

"Thank you, my dear. You held it very well. If you can get away from the commander come and see me again. There is something I'd particularly like to show you."

Outside, Tamar Kelly said, "Where are we going in that shuttle and why not use the scout car which is faster and armed?"

"Under one, *we* are not going anyplace. You are going back to the ship. Under two, everybody notices the scout car; a local craft will be less conspicuous."

"I expect you think I'm conspicuous. I could wear a Bromusian wig. There's a selection in my dressing chest. You might need a navigator."

"I'll take Sinclair."

"As of now, he couldn't find his way across an empty video booth."

"Argument will get you nowhere. You're for the ship."

But the power engineer was nowhere to be found. Vague yet polite, the hotel staff gave a number of contradictory explanations of where he was. All tallied in one respect. He had been paged, had talked with a Bromusian girl and had gone off in a white-and-gold private shuttle.

Tamar Kelly said, "It figures. Alva has him. It wouldn't do you any good if you could find him. Here I am. Take me."

Time swung the deal her way. A trip out to *Interstellar X* and a fresh start would eat into the afternoon and he wanted daylight over the area of search.

Walking out to the pickup point would use half an hour. She was dead right in one respect: he needed a second operator.

With the time disk nudging thirteen-twenty, he capitulated. "Go and get that wig. Wear something Bromusian."

Certainly they were less noticed in the street. Fletcher had a knee-length white coat with a round stand-up collar, narrow pants of the same material and his laser in a clip under his left arm. Tamar Kelly's brilliant black hair swung silkily to her shoulders, one of which was left bare by a pale apricot seethrough sari, gathered at the waist in a jade belt of interlocking double helix links.

O'Toole would have given her a Brancusi torso as a first prize for effort. She was not a Bromusian by a good sea league, having all the opulence of a 920, 610, 914 torso of her own to carry off, but she was one with the crowd, in the same idiom, but more so.

As they crossed the square into a connecting avenue she said, "How do you know they won't try again?"

"I don't. But this time we haven't signaled ahead. They don't know where we're going. Do you have a cosmetic pack?"

"Surely. Be my guest."

"Just slip the mirror out and take a good look behind."

"What am I looking for?"

"I don't know."

"That makes it easy."

"OK, leave it. Let's get on."

A navigator's flair took him through a maze of connecting ways all giving a general drift to the northern quadrant. After ten minutes he said, "Try again. Take another look in that mirror. Is there anybody you recognize?"

"Not a soul. Frankly they all look alike to me. I wouldn't know how mothers claim their own. Hold

142

it. Just a minute. Not a face, but a girdle. There's a girl just come into this stretch with a black snake-skin belt. I'd swear she was one I saw before."

"Alone?"

"No. One of three. Two men. But I don't recall that I saw them before."

They were passing through a Venusberg of erotic art, thoughtfully laid out by the city fathers to raise the morale of the afternoon strollers. Fletcher leaned casually on a transparent peach whose center stone had swollen to fill the form with a heroic Gothic ass. It was an unusual artifact for the Bromusian scene and could have derived from O'Toole's fine Italian hand.

Other considerations apart, its reflective surface showed him the trio she had picked up. They had stopped twenty meters off. The girl was sitting on a high plinth and had taken off her sandals to cool her feet, which she had parked on either shoulder of one of the escorts. A pleasant domestic scene without special menace.

Fletcher strolled on, taking direction at random for the perimeter of the arena. At the boundary wall he stopped again. There was a broad circulation space and across it a market precinct at ground level under the supporting arches of an elegant office block. In Bromusian fashion, it consisted of open circular stalls with a central slot for the merchant who stood like a stud axle in the center of a colorful wheel.

Fletcher guided Tamar Kelly across, conscious of smooth skin under his hand. Passage through the pleasure garden had made a number of subliminal suggestions. He wanted to buy her an exotic trifle and charge it to his expense account.

It was easy to circulate and face the road. The trio had crossed farther along and were sorting through

143

a tray of armlets, with the girl trying them on for size.

This time there was no doubt. Tamar Kelly said, "There they are again. She doesn't want one of those, I can tell that for a fact."

"Go farther along. Towards that line of video booths. Take your time. I'll join you in a minute."

When she was ten paces off, circulating slowly around a stall, he moved closer to the opposition. With two stalls between, he picked out a silver gilt bracelet with a motif of leaping gazelles and handed it to the salesman.

Under cover of searching for his wallet, he broke the butt of his laser and slipped out a slim three-centimeter cylinder which he cupped in the palm of his hand.

When the purchase was made, the trio had moved up and the girl was watching Tamar's progress along the stalls.

Fletcher nipped the cylinder with his thumbnail and let it fall to the tiled floor. He went on towards the trio, changed his mind, turned on his heel and followed Tamar, counting slowly in his head.

At ten there was a sharp crack and black smoke jetted from between the stalls. Circulation fans helped it along. Before he caught up with the girl there was a black curtain across the space. A quick reactor shoved in a fire call-button and a musical wail started up.

Fletcher said, "Hold your breath and follow me."

Instant chaos filled the set. With Bromusians milling every which way, there was nobody to watch them cover their faces and walk into the smoke as the posse, picking up its feet, broke through in the opposite direction.

144

Ten minutes later they were opening the hatch of O'Toole's shuttle.

Tamar Kelly said, "I've only just worked that one out. Going back on their side was very smart. You've missed your vocation."

Accepting a compliment with good grace is always a problem for a modest man. He waited until they were airborne and the autopilot was asking traffic control for a place on the seaboard freeway. Then he dug in his pocket and fished out the bracelet.

"Compensation for the loss of your dog."

"A present. You've bought me a present. It's *beautiful*, Dag."

Less inhibited, she clipped it on and wound the decorated arm around his neck.

The shuttle picked up the all clear, rose into the high transcontinental lane and accelerated away for the distant sea. On its console an illuminated strip added its gloss. *Art is long, life is short.*

It figured.

VIII

Medoc's social smile would have gone a long way to disarm any other ethnic type but the metropolitan security controller, Dagan, being a fellow Bromusian, could judge it at its value and had to bat with the handicap of a niggling doubt about his physical safety.

"It was totally unexpected, excellency. The three operators are very experienced, but they were taken completely by surprise. But there is no doubt we shall pick them up again. Every precinct is on alert."

"Are you sure they are still in Tregasid?"

"No hire service has reported in and no private shuttle has been taken."

"You are sure of that?"

"It was the first line of inquiry, excellency."

"I hope you are right."

A practical psychologist, the security satrap put the ball in the president's court. "What is your thinking, excellency? Do you have any suggestion which we could follow?"

Medoc clapped his hands softly and a girl in an electrum g-string and a navel jewel appeared with eager zeal. On the home front he was a traditionalist and preferred to see at a glance that the domestic staff was unhampered by hidden shotguns or whatever.

"Where is my daughter?"

"In her apartment, excellency."

"Is the Earthman still with her?"

"Yes, excellency."

"Tell her that I want to see him."

"There is a blue light glowing above her door. She will not like to be disturbed."

"You may use the personal call unit to speak to her. He is to be brought here through the private corridor. She is to enter first. Is that clear?"

"Very clear, excellency."

Sinclair himself was far from clear when Alva, twined around him in a supple knot and all systems go, drew clear and lay flat on her back staring into the reflective canopy over her play bed.

She appeared to be listening to something and small white teeth chewed at her lower lip in annoyance. It was inconvenient news.

Aiming to take a bite at the nearest ear to break the spell, Sinclair rolled smartly her way and found

146

he was on empty ground. She had slipped lithely out of the nest and was standing half a meter off, dividing her hair into two modest plaits.

A puzzled engineer, he asked, "What is it?"

"There is a message for me."

"Can't it wait?"

"Don't worry. We will return."

"We?"

"Yes. My father has an urgent problem."

"I have an urgent problem."

"You Earth people think only of pleasure. Be quick. He is not a good one to keep waiting."

She was already twisting into her notional sari and the temperature drop was enough to remind Sinclair that he was on a mission. It was the first time for some hours that he had managed a coherent thought beyond Alva and it sobered him enough for him to check around for his laser.

Already at the door, tapping a slim foot on the deep pile carpet, Alva said, "Quickly. You can come back for anything you have mislaid. We must hurry."

On second thought, he reckoned it would not be any advantage to have it. Deep in the presidential lodge he could only rely on his status as a visitor. But it was a straw in the wind and he was seeing Alva in a new light. From any angle she was physically incredible, but now he recognized that he knew nothing about her at all. She was alien, on a different frequency. She could be no more than a subtly fashioned android. He had projected Earth values where they had no reference or meaning.

It was a lot to think through in a short space and he was occupied with it when they reached the end of a wide connecting corridor. He could see a slice of Medoc's large shapeless drawing room through a decorated arch.

Alva, who had been at his side with a warm hand on his arm, quickened her pace and was through first, gaining a couple of meters into the room as though eager to see the head of the house.

Sinclair reached the threshold and saw the room in a brief flash, with Medoc himself and an erect uniformed Bromusian standing fifteen meters off beside a table littered with white figurines.

A fine spray from a concealed nozzle in the lintel sent a damp cloud around his head and the sudden smell of a wet dog. He dropped forward with the picture of the room clear and hard-edged like a well-lit photograph etched on his retina in full color.

It was still there to confuse him when he opened his eyes ten minutes later. He had time to see that Alva had stopped her forward run and was watching him without any surprise. No e.s.p. was needed to make it crystal clear that she knew all about it. She was watching him fall with no more than a prudent housewife's concern for the safety of the soft furnishing.

The image faded, but he was still focusing on Alva. She was so close that he could see the fine grain of the skin on her chest and was adjusting something out of sight over his head.

He tried to move his hands to grab her shoulders and ask what time it was, but there was discontinuity between the willing mind and the agent. Although he could see and hear and smell the *noa noa* of the smooth skin centimeters from his face, there was no joy. His battery was flat.

Effort brought beads of sweat to his forehead and he heard his own labored breathing as though it belonged to somebody else.

Alva said, as though to a stranger, "Relax. You

have been given a very selective drug. Certain nerve centers have been isolated."

Rolling his eyes for maximum scan, Sinclair established that he was lying at a forty-five degree angle on a padded board that dropped from the wall to the floor. Above his head on the wall itself was some kind of telemetry spread.

He was in a small room, perhaps ten meters square tiled in pale green with a single ceiling port directly over his trundle bed. The facing wall had a shifting translucent area as though the material had gone soft at that point. As he looked at it, there was a change in texture. The green hue was concentrating itself in deeper whorls, leaving clear ragged patches of infinite distance as though there were rents in the fabric of the world through which all living things could drain out.

He was used to space both as a theory and as a practical reality surrounding a hurrying starship, but this was something else: it was emptying his mind.

There were other people about; Medoc himself and the man who had been standing with him, two, perhaps three others busy at a console that ran the length of the right-hand wall. Alva had moved out of sight.

Then there was only himself. His head was filling all the space there was. He was a single eye distended with light. He was in the void and part of it with no physical identity or limiting skin.

The right-hand marker on the console said, "The subject is ready, excellency. You may put your questions."

On *Interstellar X* Jim Scullion had a number of

questions himself which were becoming an embarrassment.

In the first place he wanted to know where Fletcher was. A second starship had homed on the spaceport and had been berthed less than a hundred meters away. When the coolant cleared it was revealed as a Scotian frigate, though it was showing no military identification numerals.

In that respect it was at one with the earlier arrival which had all the earmarks of a Podargonian military unit, but had not answered recognition calls and was not showing any intention of off-loading or receiving freight.

When a tender put out from the Scotian and made its first call to the Podargonian before calling at the terminal tower, there was evidence of a link-up. It began to smell.

He called Holdbrook and Averil Marr into the command cabin for a conference.

The two ships were in plain view from the direct vision ports: wolverine additions to any sheep fold and particularly menacing here, where the spaceport was wide open and the Bromusians had no obvious defenses.

Averil Marr said, "It's their business, Jim. If they were worried they'd call I.G.O. themselves. These monkeys must be here by invitation."

"Where does that leave us?"

Holdbrook was clear on that one. "Up the creek with no paddle. This antique wouldn't last five seconds. Either one of them could see us off without getting its paint burned. When is Fletcher due back?"

"There's an arrangement for him to call the chairman. I guess he'll be along later tonight."

"Then we can only wait."

"He doesn't know about this last one. I'd like to put him in the picture."

"You can spare a navigator and still keep an operational crew."

"Taft has a full-time job with gunnery, for what its worth."

"OK, send Wilson."

"You already have Sinclair gone out of your section."

"That's all right. I can run the fall-back console from this desk. Believe me these military ships have it easy. There's no coaxing for this powerpack, it's a honey."

"OK. Call a shuttle from the terminal and I'll talk to him."

"He'll be glad to go. They've all been looking at Tregasid as if it was an angel cake."

Gary Wilson had only one question and it was not entirely in his own interest: "Sure I'd like a trip into the city, but what's the difficulty, chief? Don't we have video contact? Why don't you just talk to him on the blower?"

"I'd guess that everything we say is monitored. Except right here in the ship with the deGausser on. From his end there'd be no doubt and he might have something to pass on that he didn't want heard. Check that before you talk. Ask him if it's OK for a blue star communication. Don't go straight to the hotel. Have the shuttle drop you in town as though you were on a pleasure trip and work around to it as if on a casual visit. It's the best we can do and Christ knows you don't look like an undercover agent."

It was eighteen hundred on the nose with Tregasid softening in outline at the onset of dusk when Wilson's shuttle hovered at the main hatch to take him off. A stocky powerful youngster with a prematurely spreading forehead and a thick black spade beard to compensate, he swung himself in beside the pilot and said, "Anywhere in the pleasure precinct, Bud. I have a six-hour pass to catch up with my youth."

Whatever came out through the Bromusian's transducer, it brought a knowing smile which would have been a leer on any less urbane face and the shuttle arrowed off.

Watching from the scanner, Averil Marr said thoughtfully, "I hope he'll be all right."

The same thought had occurred to Scullion, but in the interests of crew morale he said, "Sure he'll be all right. He has a lucky aura. His kind always fall on their feet."

The boy himself, dropped on a broad sidewalk outside the sugary pink facade of the Bromusian equivalent of a Bunny Club, reckoned that staying on his feet would be a full-time chore.

More interested in a symbolic gesture than their Earth counterparts, the hospitable girls in the lobby who competed for the privilege of leading him in by the hand had reduced their costume to two floppy ears on a headband and a five-centimeter-diameter fluffy button stuck by a skin adhesive at the coccyx.

The ongoing decor beyond flimsy hangings of black lace was either a warren or a womb with deep red glistening walls that pulsated at a slow heartbeat. His entourage, thinned down to three, led him through a maze of alcoves to an empty quarter. Light drifted through every color sequence, exaltogens filtered into the air change, music was stereo-beamed to play as though by spontaneous creation in the very cavity of his inner ear.

Direction was gone, will was almost gone. If he wanted to get out he reckoned he would need a good guide. But then it was a perfect cover. Half an hour or so would establish his motive for a visit to the capital, then he could go on and find Fletcher.

The left-hand marker who was delicately stroking his beard showed the high cosmopolitan standard of the firm by speaking in English: "Eet teekles."

"It was devised with that function in mind."

"Deevised what is that deevised?"

"Never mind. You'll just have to take my word. Now steady. Steady. Just let's explore one avenue at a time and keep our cool."

Navigating on compass bearings and dead reckoning like any ancient mariner, Dag Fletcher judged the island to be a hundred and fifty kilometers ahead.

A hundred meters below the hurrying car, the sea was uniform as a solid zicon crystal, light levels were falling and the glow from the console was isolating them in a private capsule.

Tamar Kelly, who had not spoken for some time, felt all the pressure of it. In some ways the set was more alien than deep space and she was less sure of her role.

She said, "I don't like the sea. At least not the middle of the sea. Any sea actually. Not just this one. I was brought up on a farm with hills around, solid buildings that looked as though they'd been there forever. White fences and a horse called Grandee. I suppose I like my feet on solid ground."

Fletcher had a flashback of a girl riding in slow motion around a paddock on a black horse with a white blaze, ginger hair in a long ponytail, an indistinct figure calling from the house.

He said, "Grandee was a black horse."

"That's right. How did you know that? Don't tell me you've picked up this e.s.p. thing." Her voice slowed and tailed off. For a brief spell she was in Fletcher's head herself. There was a jumble of bizarre imagery: her own face was there, the clearest picture in a long gallery, with a deserted starship, the cindery black plain of an asteroid, a white tunnel shrouded in mist, endless bric-a-brac lodged in the holograph structure of memory, without a time-scale to give a ground plan.

Then the curtain dropped and she was on her own side of the psychic fence, seeing a hard profile as he stared in disbelief at the console.

Her quick, "What is it, Dag?" was out of date as she said it. She saw for herself that the compass strip had gone mad. If it were to be believed, the car had pivoted on its axis and was heading due south back to the mainland.

Fletcher switched in the auto fault-indicator and a succession of green telltales marched along the rim of the panel. If they were to be believed there was no mechanical failure at any point. If it were not the car, it was the place they were in; but he could not recall any entry of freak magnetic conditions in the pilotage manual for Bromius.

Outside it was darker. The horizon ahead was uniformly black except for a faint thread of pale apricot, slap on course, which was thickening all the time.

Concentrating on the problem had closed their minds for any transfer and he spoke it out loud. "We're crossing a forcefield. Not too strong or other gear would have been affected. Enough to sharpen e.s.p. Maybe that's how the Bromusian talent got started. This island could be special for them. The homeland of the culture."

"It's swung back."

It was true. The shadowy outline of land dotted with pinpoints of light had separated out in the horizon and the compass had done a turnabout to a true reading.

Floodlights turned the long promenade into bright, pink-tinged day, with rose-pink stone glowing against the sea. There were long empty quays and moles leading out like fingers. An expeditionary force could disembark. It was out of all proportion for a primitive reserve.

Tamar Kelly said, "What's it all for? Who comes here? And if they do where are they now?"

Certainly the waterfront was empty. Expensively lit to welcome a multitude, there was not a boat or a car in sight.

Fletcher planed down on the esplanade itself, jacked in the wheels and rolled them along past a continuous one-story building that ran in an unbroken line as far ahead as they could see.

After a good kilometer with no break in the facade, he stopped and shoved back the hatch. If it were illusion, he wanted to feel it with his feet and touch it with his hands.

Seen close, the building was not so uniform. There were areas where the smooth, tinted stone had a different texture.

It was warm to the touch, retaining the heat of the day like a huge storage heater. There was no problem; the section he leaned on slid evenly aside. They were access panels.

Side by side, they looked at a long lounge area with reclining seats similar to acceleration couches. Many small oval tables were dotted about. The far wall had floor-to-ceiling observation windows and arches leading out.

Tamar Kelly said, "It's a colossal reception area. Thousands could wait here and then go on through there. But for what purpose?"

"Not for a long stay. An overnight stop, then away again. Some kind of ceremony, I'd guess. And with this provision something that a whole lot of Bromusians do together and don't talk about."

"Unless it's just a holiday place. A month-end affair. There's a lot of movement to the coast at the month-end. Maybe we've gotten to the wrong island. I don't see any unspoiled primitives living undisturbed with this lot."

Fletcher had a passing impulse to pick her up and carry her over the threshold, suppressed it and settled for taking her hand. It was smooth and warm and companionable. They walked across the floor to the far windows in silence and looked out.

There was a five-meter strip of ashlar, then a wide road of beaten earth that could be fifty meters along. On the far side, it was edged by a solid wall of foliage, mainly broad yellow leaves, but interspersed with dark liana and the red asterisks of some flowering plant.

Tamar Kelly said, "Whatever they come for they go along that path. It's a processional way."

She need hot have said it. The same idea had risen in his head. "Wait here. I'll get the car. Lift it over and we'll follow along."

He was less than two minutes and found her standing in the center of the unpaved way. When he called out from the open hatch she did not move and he had to get out.

There was a curious sense that the light stopped at the edge of the ashlar and that the long avenue generated its own darkness. He said sharply, "Tamar," and she looked at him as though for the first time, moistening her lips with the tip of her tongue, brown eyes suddenly bright and hard. He had the feeling that if she had a knife she would have used it to attack.

It was true. The eyes told him that he had homed on a plain fact. Feinting a turn away, he dipped his shoulder, caught her in a comprehensive grip and lifted her off the ground. Before she could develop an effective counter she was over the rim of the hatch and pinned to the front squab.

Tension drained away. He felt her body go slack and cautiously loosened his grip.

Husky voice lower than usual in register, she said, "I'm sorry. Something happened to me. I wanted to kill you. Why should I want that? It's the very opposite of the way I feel."

Fletcher considered it. On the rebound from the experience she was wide open, vulnerable, without defenses. He was getting a green light, a blank check. But given the circumstances he would have to ignore it or he could not live with himself thereafter.

He put a hand on either side of her head, fingers probing under the mass of fine silk. Leaning into the cab he homed with precise component orientation on her open mouth, for a count of three. Then he said, "Shift over. The sooner we sort this one out the better. I noticed as I crossed the roof the compass went all to hell. It's another electrical field. Plays havoc with the synapses. There's some screening in the car, though. You'll be all right now."

He took it slowly, folding the skids and dropping the shuttle's six wheels. Left and right the scenery was unchanged, a continuous ashlar strip with the open rear of the caravanserai and the long back-cloth of jungle waiting for a Rousseau to paint in a frieze of monkeys.

After two kilometers there was a new feature. The road went on in the same way but another similar road made a T junction with it. This one was twice the width, edged with jungle on both sides. It was the main path to which the others were tributaries.

Tamar said with conviction, "They come from the reception areas either way and meet here. Two streams of hurrying excited people. Here they join together in one immense throng and go forward into the jungle. It isn't like the Bromusians. I always said they were too good to be true. Whatever they do is violent, I know that. It isn't helping us to find out about *Two Nine*. This is something they wouldn't want a stranger to know about."

"You want out?"

"Certainly I want out, but I know I'll wonder what was at the end of the road for the rest of time. And so will you. Just let's be quick."

Fletcher turned into the main highway. Here there were no lights and the car's single searchlight cut a swath down the center, leaving the jungle edges in shadow.

It was another full kilometer before there was any development; by that time there was room on the open road to accommodate the population of a city.

The road ran into a vast oval arena, sloping down like a shallow bowl. In the center, on a low smooth mound, was a single gaunt tree, long dead with spiky arms in silhouette against the star map of the sky. This was the place of pilgrimage and when they climbed the mound to take a closer look at the central feature, there was no reasonable doubt it was a place of sacrifice.

Fletcher had angled the car so that its searchlight eye was beamed on the tree.

Seen close it was clearly a manmade structure

replacing an original that had lived out its natural span on the site. Two meters off the ground there was a broad metal collar that gripped the trunk and carried hanging chains. Each one ended in a hinged ring too roomy for a wrist, too tight for a neck. Whoever was staked out was held by the ankle.

Since the end was half a meter off floor level, he would be forced to stand his ground on one leg.

Tamar Kelly had gone on hands and knees to inspect the smooth surface of the hill. Her face, turned up in the white beam, was pale and strained. "It's channeled for drainage. The tidy-minded ghouls have it fixed for the blood to run off."

Fletcher knelt beside her. She was right. The grooves were clean and free from dust, all ready for the next session.

Something prompted him to draw his laser and test the surface. When the bright asterisk faded they were looking at a dime-sized patch of pale metal. He gave it another short burst. The metal glowed incandescent but its surface remained unpitted and intact.

"What is it, Dag?"

But she had the answer herself before he said, "There's only one substance I know that could withstand that beam. It can only be infrangom. We're standing on enough infrangom to stock the Earth space program for a decade."

He stood up and went to the tree, knocked on it with the butt of his laser and then used the beam. "The same. It's built for all time. It's fixed to outlast the jungle itself."

Using a chain, feet braced against the trunk, he walked up to the first branch and hauled himself into the crotch. From there it was plain that the stage was fully visible from all parts of the house.

Acoustics were probably OK. Every blow would sound out for all to hear. He could imagine the sea of faces turned towards the tree and the bitter agony of the victim knowing for a certainty that no power of will or prayer could stop the action.

Out on the perimeter, at right angles to the access road and continuing the long axis of the ellipse, was a narrow avenue between the trees showing up as a pale notch against the skyline.

Tamar called, "What are you doing? We should go. I hate this place. It feels evil. Please, let's go."

Facing the trunk for a full-arm drop, he saw that the hollow crown was a shadowy chamber with a jumble of objects thrown in at random. He stretched in and drew one out. Of all things it was a conical hat with a small brim, brownish, plaited straw by texture. He shoved it back and took another. It was much the same. Ritual habit to do with the ceremony. A third dip brought up a changeling and he put it over his shoulder before he dropped down to join her.

Identification was quick and indignant. "That's my lucky dog. How would it get in there?"

The question hung about unanswered. Whatever good fortune it brought to its owner, it's own ration had run out. One of its forelegs had been wrenched off and its head was permanently twisted to one side. Once it had looked spry and depraved; now it looked dejected and depraved.

Fletcher handed it over and put his hands on her shoulders. It was a warm night but she was shivering in her sari. He bent his arms and she had to move her feet to keep her balance.

The dog was between them and when she let it fall it was a token of goodwill. Oscillation was damped down by pressure. A shiver would have to work at it to get started. Her hands moved slowly along his arms and made out with fingers laced behind his head.

As an optimistic statement of intent it went some way to purge the evil of the place.

When she could speak she said, "I think better of this sacred bough bit, but I still don't like it."

"OK. There's just one other thing to check, then we'll go back. I believe I know now what Izod found. The ethnology angle never seemed very sufficient for an assassination. Bromusians might be sensitive, but not to that extent. He found infrangom. Which is very curious because I happen to know there's no deposition of a strike on I.G.O. files. Where or how can be worked out. But somebody believed it was knowledge he shouldn't pass on."

"And now we have it?"

They went down the slope into the glare of the searchlight hand in hand at arm's length, making a royal progress of it.

Fletcher lifted the car a meter and swung it slowly through three hundred and sixty degrees with the bright lance throwing a ragged spot on the perimeter of the vast clearing. The three outlets were all. One they had seen. He ran for the left-hand axis.

Unlike the entry road it was paved with the familiar pink stone in meter-square slabs, flat and straight as a die, edged by deep culverts to stop the march of the forest and drain its surface. It could have been newly put down or it could be ancient as the planet's culture.

Kilometer after kilometer it was a uniform gash across the center of the island. When Fletcher judged they must be getting close to the coast it ran out suddenly onto a paved circular apron surrounded by a waist-high parapet.

He turned the car for the trip back and dipped the headlight with a wide beam to show up the surface.

Tamar said, "It's a diagram. A planetary system. Bromius?"

Heavy grooves divided the circle into four quadrants. Where the diameters crossed in the center was a large two-meter-radius bas relief of a planet. From the etched equatorial landmass it was Bromius and no other. Seven moons were shown in orbit: six plate-size, simply carved on the pink stone; the seventh was smaller, maybe ten centimeters across, but it was given special treatment.

The seventh moon stood out as a hemisphere, multi-faceted, gathering light like an immense ruby.

They left the car and stood over it.

"There's one thing I don't understand, Dag."

"Only one? You're lucky."

"Well at this time, one in particular. You remember the charts we used to come in. There's no mention of seven moons. Six is the figure and I'd say the layout on this diagram was absolutely accurate. On a two-dimensional figure, they'd appear this way. Four bunched, two in the third quadrant. Where does this joker fit? Who provides detail for the manual?"

"Local surveyors in an advanced culture. Otherwise an I.G.O. survey team. There'd be no advantage in suppressing any detail."

"Could it refer to historic truth? Originally there could have been a seventh. Now its a mythological thing. For that matter anybody finding a Ptolomaic map would get a slanted view of Earth."

Fletcher was on hands and knees, feeling the surface of the stone. It was smoother than any yet. Me-

162

tallic. Metal finished to resemble stone. Infrangom again for a sure bet. Palms pressed down, he could feel a faint vibration. Ear pressed to the ground, he listened for it.

Tamar Kelly cleared a swath of hair from her left ear and joined him at it. A more delicate instrument, she was first to identify a cause. "It's hollow. There's machinery down there. Rotary. Not on load. Waiting to be put to work."

She squatted back on her heels, thighs taut and comely, hair surging elastically from the move, a shapely rabbit for any bizarre grove.

For the moment the sheer incongruity of it distracted Fletcher. She transformed the set into an ordinary thing, being herself the master product of evolution in this or any other place. Then he was hauling her to her feet and hurrying her to the waiting car.

Some pieces had snapped into a pattern. The circular area was no more than a covering hatch for a silo below. The finely dovetailed quadrants were designed to open like the petals of a flower. It was no place to be when the operator decided to go into countdown.

When they reached the central grove there was no change. It was empty as though it had never been used and would never be used again. He hesitated at the central mound and Tamar made it easy for him. "I know you want to see what's at the other end of the line. Don't mind me. I agree we ought to find out for the record. But as quick as you can. It's beginning to give me the green creeps."

Knowing roughly what to expect shortened the journey. The trip-distance gauge said that the two arms were symmetrical, but it seemed half as long before the searchlight bored out to a circular well at the end of the burrow. Having seen one they'd seen them all. It was identical. There was the same ruby moon and the same carefully incised planetary system.

Fletcher did not stop. He went around in a tight turn and drove back down the alley.

Within the half-hour, he was lifting the shuttle over the long line of the marshaling hospice and sitting it down on the quayside close to the sea. At the same time every light on the long quay blanked out.

From being absorbed in the bright floods the car's single beam flared out again until it was lost in distance.

The Bromusian time disk on the console was metering Dusk 4 on the nose. Due south, over the sea, one of the six regular moons shoved its full circle over the horizon as though on cue. There would be enough light for the clientele to find their way along the earth road.

It was moving visibly, already clear of the skyline when a second larger orb, green-tinged with a brown central feature like a ragged trapezoid, lifted itself on the set twenty points west.

That was the way it would be: house lights down; nature itself putting up the props; a great concourse of people suddenly plunged in darkness stumbling out onto the track with the floor of sophistication whipped smartly from under their feet.

There was no compulsion either. That was the secret of the empty quayside. No marshals or instructions or resident staff. It was a voluntary act. Every man was reacting to his own inner compulsion.

Whatever was done was a kind of race therapy which the people turned to instinctively like lemmings rushing over a cliff into the sea.

They were both silent as Fletcher lifted the car, slewed it through ninety degrees and accelerated away. Below them the ridged sea was iridescent.

Ignoring the compass which was swinging every which way, Fletcher locked on the autopilot at maximum ceiling and thrust. He reckoned that there was no risk of missing the continental landmass that crosssed their bow beyond the horizon.

They could have been out from a starship waiting for them in a parking orbit over an empty world.

Tamar Kelly slipped out of her sandals and curled around on the squab, leaning his way, sure of a welcome.

Fletcher gathered her in, his data acquisition network going into overload. The physical equation was complex: a modulus of elasticity to figure, thermal agitation, a subtle pollen count, hair in a smooth fall over his arm, eyes dark, almost all pupil and giving a value as a key to all coordinates.

She was on his side in this and any foreseeable situation. At the heart of the hurrying module there was a nucleus to defy time.

IX

The sleeping human head had numbed his right arm from the shoulder. But Fletcher was glad of its positive weight. She was solid and tangible as the Cheshire farm she had been telling him about. He knew his personal flaw as a weaver of fantasy. Tamar walked on the ground. She was inside his barrier reef as a three-dimensional object, making a physical dent.

Tregasid's lights were dead ahead, an aurora arching across the skyline. He dropped to the lowest traffic lane and reduced speed. Then, as the first suburbs reared slab-sided from the open plateau, he came down on the surface road, switched to wheels and moved on.

The change in motion wakened her. She turned her head in the crook of his numb arm and looked first at the console like a good astronaut, then at the windshield.

"Dag. You've let me sleep through. You should have had me take a spell. What do we do now?"

"Leave the shuttle where we found it. Then a brisk walk. Looking as though we've been on some scheme of pleasure."

"That won't be difficult. I like being with you."

"That's pillow talk and the good moment has gone. Life is real and life is earnest, young Kelly."

Arms went around his neck and her forehead pressed briefly against his. "Now I know how people get to be senior controllers. They have a hard and loveless streak. OK. Be like that. I'll go talk to my poor dog."

The parking lot was still half full. Bromusians played late. Coming from a great distance with new and dangerous knowledge in their heads, they might have expected the set to have changed. But the few strollers in the avenues had their own fish to fry. There was no challenge.

Fifty meters before the last connecting way opened to the main square, Fletcher stopped under a tree. He had left it late on the sound principle that if there were to be argument it were better short.

"It could be that Medoc has shown his hand. They could have been looking for us. What we know must go back to the ship for onward report. The scout car is on the terrace. To the left of the porch as I recall. When we leave the trees, I'll walk straight across the square. When I get halfway over, you start. Filter round the outside. Take the car and go back to the ship. Tell Scullion what we saw and then call Europeah Space and report it there. Understood?"

"Understood. But suppose they're waiting for you on the porch? I could pick you up. It's an armed car."

Fletcher put both hands on her shoulders. She was anxious for him and it was a novel situation to be in. "Not, repeat not. Whatever you see or hear you do nothing about it. Yours is the tough part and I'm sorry about that. You have to get yourself in one piece to *Interstellar X*. OK?"

"If you say so."

Agreement was reluctant, but once given he knew she would carry it out.

He bent his head quickly. Found her mouth, an open anemone O; saw in the long tunnel of his mind the possible future they might have; slammed the door on it.

"Let's go."

He walked out from the end of the avenue as if he had been alone. Without looking back.

Tamar Kelly watched his tall figure withdrawing across the square and felt more alone than anytime she could remember.

Mathematics gave her a focus. She chose grid lines: one from the center of the tower block way over on the right, running to a group of statuary with a circle of maenad dancers around a fluted column; another from a potted shrub to the right-hand corner of the State Guest House itself. They were so real in her mind's eye that she was surprised when he walked through the intersection without falling on his face.

With her dog under her arm she set off under a

curving arcade that ended in a stretch of formal garden heavy with the scent of frangipani.

Except for occasional couples on the discreetly sited stone seats, she had it to herself.

A girl angling around to put an agreeable bite on her escort's neck watched her pass over his shoulder, saw the mutilated dog, shuddered delicately and closed her eyes. When she reopened them Tamar Kelly was gone, but some of the magic had drained out of the night and she asked to be taken home.

Tamar Kelly reached the end of the garden area and found herself cut off by a shoulder-high containing wall of black basalt with a long frieze in bas relief. Over it she could see the parking lot a hundred meters distant, with open ground between except for a floodlit fountain sending up streamers of orange and blue water.

The nudge of a sixth sense made her look around. Three parallel lanes led to the path she was on. Every last one had a uniformed Bromusian guard halfway along, moving silently as if on foam-rubber feet.

Mountaineering in a sari was no good. She shrugged out of it, pitched her dog ahead and jumped athletically for the barrier, using biological features of the sculpture as convenient foothold.

The center guard, coordinator of the enterprise, called something sharp in Bromusian. It could have been appreciation of the star-burst motif on her neat triangular briefs, but she did not wait to find out. Scooping up her mascot, she was off to a sprint start over the tesserae.

Earth physique was coming out well. A quick look over her shoulder at the edge of the parking lot told her that she had actually gained a few meters.

Threading a way through the parked shuttles lost

some time. One guard veered off and was on the shorter leg of a triangle running her down as she reached the hatch. Slamming it open gave him five meters. He was near enough to see that his face was full of confidence and open malice which she had never expected to see in a Bromusian.

She swung her dog like a bolas and let go.

Hands clawing at his neck, he lost rhythm doing a complicated dance step to keep balance.

Needle cold, Tamar Kelly ran through the starting sequence and felt the scout car come to life. Two meters off the deck in a crash vertical start, she felt the sudden list as a guard grabbed for the port skid.

She killed vertical boost and surged forward savagely in a move that would slap the human pendulum into the side of the next car in line and felt the trim go stable as he prudently chose dishonor.

Circling the square, she could see that Fletcher was gone. They had been too optimistic. Medoc must have picked up the trail as soon as they entered Tregasid. That meant there would be a reception committee in the hotel.

But the man had said go. He was right. She fed in more power until the needle was edging into the red quadrant and the scout car was streaking over the silent city on a direct line for the spaceport with its I.G.O. pennant straining stiff as a metal cutout.

Fletcher entered the lobby pushing the swing panel with his left hand and holding his laser ready for use under his mandarin jacket.

Except for a clerk at the desk killing the boredom of the middle watch with a game of three-dimensional solitaire, there was no one in sight. Maybe he had been overanxious at that.

He went for the elevator, veered off halfway with a change of plan and approached the sportsman.

"Have there been any calls for me?"

The man stopped with a hand poised in midair, carefully put the piece on the desktop and appeared to give the matter all attention.

"One, I think, commander. Early in the evening."

He worked busily at an auto secretary. An illuminated slot on his console whipped through a number of entries and stopped at one. A well-modulated voice spoke out of the woodwork in confirmation: "Commander Fletcher is requested to contact his ship. Message originates from Captain Scullion. Rated important."

"Would you have told me if I hadn't asked?"

"There is a printout beside your video in your room, commander. If you wish to call now I will make the link."

"I'll do that."

By this time Tamar should be on the way. If she made a first call to the command cabin, he could say sleep well or whatever formula you used to a newly acquired hostage to fortune.

That was cynical and untrue. She was her own woman, no kind of hostage. An addition, not a distraction.

He shoved open the door of his suite. It was in darkness. The leaf screen over the long window was shut. He pressed a stud beside the lintel for houselights and the room was the busiest square of Bromius he had seen in a long night.

Dagan, the metropolitan security controller, had a chair in the center of the floor and was sitting erect, elbows chocked on the arms, fingertips meeting, thumbs gently stroking the underside of his chin. He looked relaxed and free from any fear that the

170

returning wayfarer would stand on his citizen's rights and throw him out.

Confidence had a reasonable base. Spaced out around the walls in a supporting role, a section leader and eight troopers of the security force had carbines lined up on Fletcher's sternum. If they all fired at once, which they seemed anxious to try as an exercise in group participation, he reckoned his head would drop into his pelvic girdle for lack of intermediate support.

The man nearest the door, without disturbing his aim, stretched out a long arm and closed it to keep out the draught.

Fletcher stood still, keeping his hands from his laser, and waited for the good word.

Dagan said conversationally, "We have been waiting to see you for some time, commander. Would you care to say where you have been?"

The tone gave away that it was all one to the speaker. He could find out and would do so; but he was ready to hear it volunteered as a starting point for the dialogue.

Keeping an image of Tamar Kelly's head in the forefront of his conscious mind, which was not too difficult since it was well and away more satisfactory than any head on the set, Fletcher said frankly, "You have a very fine city. Some fascinating entertainments. If I stayed long I guess I'd be applying for citizenship. Who are you and why do you ask?"

"I will ask the questions, commander. However, I should tell you that I am Dagan, controller of the metropolitan security force. I ask because I want to know."

"You are aware that I have diplomatic status as an executive officer of the I.G.O. military command?"

"I am aware of it, commander, and it does not bother me. Neither does the presence of your obsolescent corvette in our spaceport. Any meance there might have been from that quarter is now neutralized by the presence of our allies. Your ship is in balk."

"You will have to have very important reasons for this action. As of now you have a certain advantage. Tomorrow or the next day, figuratively speaking, an I.G.O. taskforce will home on Tregasid with an account to settle."

"I think not, commander. I think not. They would only do that if you were to make a report which would bring them. At this moment our Laodamian friends have arranged a forcefield which puts your ship out of communication. Eventually that will be lifted and your voice will be heard again, telling your organization that you are satisfied that the loss of your other ship was an accident. Also that faults have developed on your ship which call for an extended stay in port. After that, you will not be heard of again. Your crew after being subjected to certain therapy procedures will fly out the ship. They will all tell the same story which will satisfy every reasonable inquiry."

"Surely this depends on my cooperation?"

"That would be helpful, of course. But no. It is immaterial whether you go along with us or not. The end result will be the same."

Habit died hard. Fletcher found he was working out the angles. Reaction time being what it was, there would be a gap before a signal from Dagan could be recognized and coded into a stimulus to bend a trigger finger. His own move would have one less process and would be that much shorter. He could certainly kill Dagan before the slugs tore into him. Was that what he ought to do? There would be no question then of using him for any purpose.

Dagan had stopped stroking his chin and was still as a stone figure. He had followed the argument as if it had been printed out on a balloon over Fletcher's head.

When he spoke it was breathed out very quietly so as not to force the action and the message appeared to rise as a new thought inside the Earthman's head.

"It is just possible that you could do that. But there is a saying on your planet—where there is life there is hope. Never despise a cliche; it has a kernel of truth. Nothing is certain except death and a forward thinker delays that as long as possible."

Dag Fletcher recognized that the voice was not his own. He also understood that he no longer had a choice. All possible paths had brought him to this point. Either he acted on principle or he was nothing, an android, a straw man.

He saw Dagan's eyes show sudden fear as the security man correctly interpolated the omega point on the graph of decision.

As Dagan's left hand sliced down to the arm of his chair Fletcher was moving in a controlled dive for the man's feet.

Overhead the carbines fired as one. Chest-high, a ragged half-meter hole appeared in the door.

Tracking around for a second shot, the firing squad had a problem. Dagan had accepted the calculated risk that he could be a victim, but the individual marksmen had to weigh the angles of what was the likely future for a trooper who shot a controller even in a good cause.

173

Dagan confused the issue by trying to stand and found himself airborne as Fletcher took him by throat and crotch and swung him in a half-circle.

The section leader, voice notched up with emotion, rattled out an order and the detail dropped their carbines and jumped for the busy center.

In a poor situation, Fletcher reckoned he had one advantage. He knew who was on his side.

Numbers hampered the Bromusians and their lightweight physique was not geared for a saloon brawl.

Swinging Dagan like a sickle, Fletcher cleared himself a space, pitched the man clear, dropped on one knee to bring one who had jumped on his back over his head and went from a sprint start for the bathroom.

He was inside with the hatch slammed shut and bolted before anybody could pick up a carbine.

There was a louvered window high up on the outside wall. He swung an upholstered stool at it as a heavy butt splintered a panel beside the catch.

Glass shards tearing at his skin, he was through above the connecting verandah. He dropped down, crossed to the baluster and swung over it without a check. At full arms' stretch from the cornice, he could feel the rail of the verandah below with his toes.

The courtyard was fifty meters of freefall at his back and his hands suddenly began to sweat. But he had no grip to get back even if he wanted to. He willed himself to fall forward, felt his whole foot meet the parapet and ducked in split-second reactions to fall over the parquet in an acrobat's roll. But it was a method that he knew he could not use all the way down the tower block.

The suite was identical with the one above and the leaf blind was shut, but a glow behind it told that

174

the owner was still using the hours for which he must give account to some useful purpose.

Fletcher tried the door. It was locked. His laser had stayed with him in the band of his pants and he used it to burn out the wards.

Inside he was in Arabian Nights territory. Three Bromusians sitting up in a circular bed, the twin of Tamar's, watched him cross their carpet with round, astonished eyes.

If he had been wearing a hat he would have raised it in respect. As a substitute he said in speech tones to the nearer of the two girls, "Please don't bother about me, I can see myself out."

Coat ripped in tatters, blood streaking his skin, face stony with effort, the polite formula did nothing for them. E.s.p. making for a group decision, they vanished under the sheet in a complicated knot like so many gophers.

Fletcher soldiered on into the corridor and ran for the elevator trunk. Waiting for a cage he leaned his back on the housing, ready to drop any guard using the stairway.

He had a count of ten to think it through before the doors sliced open. In a racing analysis, he saw that Dagan had it sewn up. With other military units on the pad, *Interstellar X* was effectively cornered. Eventually Scullion would have to evacuate.

Bitterly he blamed himself for undervaluing the Bromusians. No doubt they had other tricks in their locker. There would be some way of beating the ship's screens and working on the crew from inside their own heads.

God, how complacent could you get? And of all people with his experience of the bizarre cultures of the galaxy, he should have known better. Instead of doing the job he was paid for he had been chasing a girl like any first mission subaltern. By doing that he had sold the pass and put her at risk with the rest.

There was only one possibility as of now. Medoc himself was politically aware enough to know the issues that were at stake. He should get to Medoc and make him see that he was starting a fire that he would not be able to control.

Given a course of action, his computer flipped into gear like an autopilot.

Another cage was homing on the landing, coming from the floor above. He shifted around to face the door as it opened, thumbing the laser stud for a wide-angle beam.

There was a ten-centimeter gap and he had his fist through, shooting point blank at four guards too closely packed to swing their carbines. When the panel was fully open, they were standing like stone figures poised to take a step.

He leaned in, switched them on a nonstop trip to the penthouse and joined his own waiting cage.

The lobby was still empty. All lights except the strip over the desk had been dimmed. The clerk had gotten himself to an impasse in his solitary chore and was peering moodily at his illuminated cube.

Fletcher was in front of him before his hand could reach the alarm and took him by the slack of his tunic.

It was all very unfair but the just had to suffer with the unjust, and who on Bromius belonged to the party of the first part he would need a crystal ball to find out.

Making it slow and clear, Fletcher said, "Where is Controller Dagan's car?"

No e.s.p. was needed to read the message that truth was balanced against survival.

"It has been brought round to the porch, commander."

"How many men?"

"Two, commander. The pilot and one other."

"Controller Dagan wants them up aloft. Get them. Don't take no for an answer. I'll watch you and be sure that if you say anything else, you'll be the first to go."

Fletcher waited beside the door and watched him cross the porch to a long red-and-green shuttle with Dagan's personal pennant hanging limply from an aerial stub.

The man was doing his best, hands moving in an eloquent mime as he told his tale.

Then two men climbed from the open hatch and joined him on the paved court. They were clearly reluctant to leave the car and Fletcher was weighing distances, judging that it was extreme range for the wide angle stunning beam and coldly reckoning that in five more seconds he would shoot to kill.

At four, his thumb was on the stud and they began to walk.

Flat to the wall, he let the clerk go by and walk six meters into the lobby with the two guards close together just behind him; then he shot with clinical accuracy for the three heads.

The shuttle's motor was running. There was a temptation to head for the ship. Scullion had no military experience and could not be expected to fight off a professional attack. But he knew that his first decision was the right one. Medoc was the key figure in the local equation.

He was fifteen meters off the deck rising fast when the remnants of Dagan's cutting-out party showed up on the step.

177

Reacting automatically, he slammed the clumsy car into a sideslip and the scattered volley that should have raked the underside ricocheted from the port bulkhead.

It was his night for glass. Fist-sized shards from the plexidome fell around him on the squab. The slipstream of warm scented air shoved him down into the spring seat as he stormed out of the square at maximum thrust.

The presidential lodge was a blaze of light lit from floods around the perimeter of its trim park. It was like diving into a bright pool.

He touched down twenty meters from the porch and was on his way before the car had risen on its jacks.

There was an all-night porter at a horseshoe console in the reception area and two security guards in boxlike body armor on either side of the door, sitting in swivel chairs at duplicate perimeter defense desks with scanner screens that must have monitored him all the way. Transparent shields swung with the seats as they pinpointed him in crossfire.

Recognition gear had accepted Dagan's car, but his own personal appearance weakened credibility. Even a security chief's transport could not cover for an Earthman who looked as though he had been in a losing demo.

A voice speaking from mid-distance said, "Far enough. Stand still and state your business."

"I have to see the president as a matter of urgency."

"Urgent to you or to him?"

"Urgent to every man, woman and child on Bromius. Just use some of that sophisticated gear and talk to him."

"He will not like to be disturbed at this time."

"Nobody is going to like it if I don't get to see him but quick."

The night porter had been doing a quick scan through a file and spoke inaudibly into a handset.

The disembodied voice came up with the statement, "You are Commander Fletcher of the Earth starship *Interstellar X*."

"Right. Also I.G.O. envoy. This is a political matter which the president must know about."

"Wait."

There was a three-way discussion behind the acoustic screens.

Fletcher suddenly felt very tired. He was also less sure that he had done the right thing. Medoc must be in it right up to his neck. Nothing could be said that would make him switch course at this point in time. Any minute now Dagan would pick up the trail and the chance of even talking to Medoc would be gone.

He had convinced himself that he had handed himself over for no purpose when the voice spoke again. "Your request will be allowed. Drop your handgun and stand away from it. You will be checked for other weapons."

There was nothing to be gained by keeping it. Given time the laser beam could cut through either one of the shields, but by that time the other operator would have picked his spot and cut him down.

Fletcher dropped the gun, walked two paces farther in and said, "You have decided well. The president will approve your action."

"Let us hope for your sake that it is so."

There was another stage wait. Then two more guards in the same bulky rig filed in from an arch in the left-hand wall.

The voice had a more conciliatory tone than at

any time yet when it said, "The president will see you, commander. You will appreciate that your appearance at this time is unusual. Security has to be kept. Go forward with the escort and they will take you to the president's suite. He will join you in a few minutes."

As he passed between the two swivel desks, they turned to face each other. When he was through, the talking void made a last contribution. The new friendship deal was only skin deep. "The commander is not carrying any weapon."

Fletcher spent the three minutes it took to reach the audience room going over his brief. He had to convince Medoc that self-interest lay in following the I.G.O. line. On the face of it there was no chance. A man at the top of his own heap had everything already. What made him gamble for more? A man could only use so much power. Wealth was a relative term. Security he had. Behind it all there must be a drive which only made sense to Medoc himself and to dig for it would need a couch and a dedicated analyst.

He was still pondering it when Medoc appeared in a deep blue robe with a bronze chain belt, flanked by two of the girls who seemed to fill every crevice of the lodge. Less concerned about appearances than the top man, they had only slipped on fresh leis and gentle open smiles.

Fletcher was isolated in the middle of the floor. The two guards had stationed themselves handily against the wall with bulbous blasters prominently at the ready.

Taking the initiative, Fletcher said, "It is good of you to see me at this time, president. I believe the matter is urgent. Before a point of no return is reached I must ask you to consider the course you have set."

"Sit down, commander. Osyth, Regna, see that the commander is comfortable. I am sure you believe that what you have to say is important. A drink will refresh you."

Menace was hard to see over the pale rounded gleam of Osyth's shoulder as she plumped up a cushion for the late-late guest. But Fletcher worked at it, seeing the island grove in his mind's eye and knowing for a truth that the surface show was a total mirage.

Medoc helped it along, drawing up a chair and saying, "So you wonder what reason I have for my actions. It is doubtful that you would understand if I tried to explain. Bromius was old when life on your planet was creeping painfully from the sea."

So the smooth bastard had lost no time in beaming in on the e.s.p. link. Aided and abetted by some very sophisticated hardware, no doubt. Laodamian technicians in the woodwork for a brass monkey. Any diplomat negotiating on this pad was outflanked before a delegate uttered his first expedient lie. There was no point in trying to cover. The truth anyway was the strongest possible argument.

At close range, Medoc was working the special Bromusian talent for himself. He confirmed Fletcher's thinking. "Truth has many aspects. You Earthmen have the serious flaw that you believe your own standpoint on any issue is the only one and that anyone who differs from you is either a fool or a knave. Truth is relative, like esthetics. It has its value for a particular place and a particular time."

Fletcher stopped trying to control his mind. He needed all his concentration to organize what he was going to say. There was enough distraction on the set with Osyth and Regna leaning over the back of the sofa ready for another go at smoothing his cushion.

He said, "Some values change, some endure. Some evolve in a particular place, some are universal. If you don't see that, there's nothing I can say that will change your mind. I've moved about the galaxy more than most and if I've learned nothing else I've learned that. In spite of setbacks and some planets like Scotia, there's an underlying pattern for good order, justice and social virtue. For my money the I.G.O. constitution is in line with those principles. It isn't perfect, nothing is; but it's moving in the right direction. However, you didn't leave your warm bed to hear a dissertation on philosophy, so I'll stick to certain practical issues."

"I would appreciate that." Medoc's voice had the trace of a sneer.

"OK. I believe I know the root cause of all the brouhaha. You have large deposits of infrangom on Bromius. You have reasoned falsely that your interest lies with the Outer Galactic Alliance. You have some plan for supplying these planets with strategic quantities of ore or refined metal. How you can believe that Scotia, to name only one, will work in harness with Bromius passes all belief."

"And your ship? A man with so many theories will have one about that." This time there was no mistaking the sneer and Medoc had stopped smiling.

"I wouldn't know the details, but I'd say that Izod saw what I have seen. Maybe he tried to use it as a lever to get permits for his work. Some of your smart new partners saw a way to infiltrate his research party and diverted the ship back into Bromius space. Knowing Scotians I'd say they were prepared to ditch their own people. It wouldn't surprise me if the ship was destroyed with all hands including the deluded fools who made it possible. There's a point you should take. Small scale, big scale, cut where you like, O.G.A. is a bad smell."

Even without e.s.p., Fletcher could see that he had scored a hit. Medoc had stopped sneering and was thinking about it

He was not however thinking that it was hard on the agents who had pulled *Interstellar Two Nine* off-course. He was reviewing the data to check that there were enough safeguards in the enterprise to stop any subtle ally from chiseling him out of his legitimate percentage. Reckoning that the infrangom was solidly sited on Bromusian ground and that Bromius had survived a long time in its vulnerable corner of the cosmos, he judged finally that the warning, though interesting, could be shrugged off.

It only remained to deal with this pushy Earthman who had made it all very easy by walking up and putting his head on the block.

Medoc stood up, walked to the back of his chair and rested his hands on its brocaded top rail. He was all set for a ministerial statement and made it in two parts.

"You have a certain shrewdness, commander, which is admirable in its way. Since you have made so much deduction I will tell you about your ship. What you say is substantially true. Dr. Izod was foolish enough to think he could use blackmail to forward his project. Ironically enough there was no need for his investigation. We are fully aware of the race link with Croton. Bromusians colonized Croton many millennia ago and the changes in physique which now exist are explained by the independent development of the stock under new environmental conditions."

"Galapagos with a human factor."

Medoc did not like the interruption, but inclined his head. "You are well-informed for a military man. Yes, your Darwin made some crude observations of what happens to a species when it becomes isolated in a particular place. Izod also made other discoveries which we were not anxious to have published to people who would not understand."

"Try me."

"Indeed you will be given an opportunity to see into that mystery, but all in good time. I am sure you would like to know about the ship."

The words were like so much syrup in Fletcher's ears. The warmth of the room, the even, well-modulated voice, the very softness of the cushions he was on, were combining to make it a dream sequence. There was a powerful pollen cloud at work which he had listed as the *noa noa* of his two nubile neighbors. Belatedly he reckoned he would be better standing up, but when he pushed down with his hands to heave himself forward his body seemed to have gained weight.

Straining every atom of nerve and will he forced himself forward, eyes fixed on Medoc's face, veins corded on his forehead. He made the edge, passed a point of no return in balance and dropped on his knees, head sawing left and right like a bemused dog.

Medoc had not moved. He carried on without an alternation in tone. "Your ship turned into our gravisphere as we expected it would. There is a beacon which we seldom use which overrode the local controls. It was diverted to the southern polar sea and is now lying two kilometers below surface in the Urion trench. So much for that. On the other matter you are quite right. I intend to supply infrangom to the O.G.A. states. Perhaps you have never considered the balance of power. At the moment I.G.O. is over-strong. It has everything its own way. If the Rim planets are strengthened Bromius and Croton will be at the fulcrum. We shall dictate. Indeed we would not care if the two empire-building factions destroyed each other. You are barbarians, all of you."

Fletcher used the last of the strength he had. It should have come out as a shout. But his relaxed voicebox only mustered a croak. He said in English, the only medium his failing computer had any grip on: "Whom the gods wish to destroy, they first make mad."

His arms crumpled like so much rubber hose and he fell flat on the parquet at Medoc's feet.

Medoc signaled curtly for the two guards to come forward. "Put him with the other two. All are to be kept under sedation and transported to the Island of Renewal. I will personally join in the ceremonial tomorrow night. Meanwhile I will speak to those left aboard the Earth starship. It is time they understood the position they are in."

X

A roving searchlight beam from the spaceport control tower picked up the hurrying scout car as it crossed the perimeter and locked on.

Diggory Taft at the end of a long stint in the control cabin of *Interstellar X* saw it appear iridescent as a dragonfly in the center grid of the main scanner and sensed that it was no social call. He stabbed down the general alarm and shoved over the lever which opened the docking port. At the same time he broadcast on the general net, "Scout car coming in. Looks urgent."

Consequently there was a full roll call of the depleted crew in the narrow, brilliantly lit bay to see Tamar Kelly slide back the hatch and join the company in her starburst briefs.

It was a good entrance and saved some explanation. Obviously there was trouble ashore. Hobb's appreciative whistle got him a cold glare. She ducked out of the bay saying over her shoulder, "I'll grab a suit on my way and report in the control cabin. Give me half a minute."

Even with the stop to snatch up a white drill coverall from her locker, she was not last in. As Holdbrook heaved himself ponderously over the sill, Scullion said, "Take your time, Tamar. What's it all about? Where's the commander?"

Zipping the last six centimeters to complete the conversion from an erotic object to a working astronaut taking deep breaths, she said, "We separated. He was to go back to the hotel. I was to get the information we have to the ship for onward signal. He thought they might be looking for us and I guess he was right. I only just got out from under in the car. Where that leaves him, I don't know. I believe they'd be waiting for him."

Averil Marr said, "Why the sudden change of heart? Why have they come out in the open?"

"Maybe they always intended it. What we found makes it likely. There's a multibillion cache of infrangom on an offshore island. That's at the back of it and that's the message that has to go to I.G.O."

"What has *Two Nine* to do with that? Walker wouldn't be fool enough to run infrangom out of

Bromius." Holdbrook was thinking aloud more than asking a direct question.

Scullion said slowly, "Even to know that there's infrangom here is enough. I can tell you for a fact it's never been declared. Sited so near the Rim, it's political dynamite. OK, Tamar, you can have the pleasure. Finish a heroine's run by sending the message."

"To I.G.O?"

"No. Spencer's the man. He'll see the importance of it and shift it along the channels. Also it will cause less surprise if it's monitored. We talk to European Space every day."

Tamar Kelly took her familiar desk, ran a quick check over the gear, selected the company channel and keyed in the robot caller for attention.

The rest had grouped themselves at the direct observation ports and were looking out at the dark columns of the two military ships. The Podargonian was showing lights at the waist and at the cone, but the Scotian was uniformly dark except for a phosphorescent glow at ground level and seemed to radiate the more positive menace.

Averil Marr shivered delicately and said, "I've gone off this mission and that's a fact. When can we head for home?"

With an eye on his communications expert, Scullion asked, "What's the problem? Don't they answer?"

Tamar stood up to say formally, "It's no good, captain. How they've done it I can't say, but every signal is turning back. There's a complete radio blanket on."

Hobbs was beside her in two strides to his duplicate desk. Every eye tracked his movements as he went through the repeat drill. Thirty seconds later he said heavily, "That's right enough. No joy. Any information we have is locked up in this gravisphere."

At the same time, the local video glowed with the international call sign and the transducer chattered out a half-meter of yellow tape. Holdbrook tore it off and read out: "Earth starship *Interstellar X* from Tregasid Space Control. You are not permitted to leave Bromius. Allied units have orders to destroy you if you attempt to move."

Averil Marr nearest the observation port called out, "Look at that, then. The Scotian's moving."

It was all true. Flame rolled brilliantly into the blast trenches and the dark minaret began to edge itself into the night sky.

There was no doubt either about the maneuver. She would settle in a parking orbit over Tregasid. *Interstellar X* would not make ten kilometers before she were blasted.

Scullion said harshly, "Talk to control, executive. Tell them they're putting themselves outside the law. Tell them also that any attack on the ship will bring retribution first to them."

Before Hobbs could make a move, the video was busy again. This time the text was spoken out in English by a visible straight man in a blue smock and Tamar Kelly, who had been introduced, said quickly, "That's Medoc himself."

She was just ahead of the president who announced it in confirmation. "I am Medoc, president of the council of Bromius. I will speak with the acting commander of the Earth starship."

Scullion tuned himself in and said flatly, "Captain Scullion. Go ahead."

"Three of your crew including Commander Fletcher are in my hands. They have committed serious breaches of Bromius law. What happens to them depends on your good sense and cooperation."

"I demand to speak to Commander Fletcher."

"That is not possible. Obviously you do not appreciate the position you are in. I will make any demands that are to be made. You are to leave your ship. A shuttle will be sent to take you off. All personnel will be taken to the reception area for interrogation. I have reason to believe that there is a political agent attempting to make illegal entry into Bromius. Those who are cleared will be allowed to return."

"Suppose I say no?"

"You will be unwise to say no. Bromius is not without its technology. Every hour that you delay the temperature in your ship will rise by five degrees Celsius. I will give you twelve hours by your reckoning. At the end of that time the heat will surge beyond the limits of your protective gear. I hope you will not wait until that time."

Medoc switched himself out. There was silence, underlined by the sliding click of the main chronometer. Taft said, "Can he do that, chief?"

"If he says so. He wouldn't claim something that we can easily check over the next hour and not deliver. Scullion looked at the heat gauge on his console. It was steady at 19.5 Celsius. "Sixty on that puts the suits at the top end of tolerance. We'll just have to see if he can make it stick."

"Sweat it out?"

"Right."

Scullion had both hands flat on his desk. It was a poor beginning for independent command. He came to a decision, negative but the best he could do. "That wraps it up. Stand down. For now we wait. Get some sleep. By first light we'll know whether he's bluffing."

Tamar Kelly thought she would never sleep and woke up believing it, with a dry mouth and a tropical heat in her small cabin. First thought was for Fletcher and a personal reproach that she could have been so callous as to sleep at all when he was in danger.

In the ward room extractor fans were moving the air about, but Medoc's technicians seemed to have sited a capsule of hot air around the ship. It was thirty Celsius and still rising. Holdbrook, who felt the heat, was already wearing a spacesuit with refrigeration at its first setting.

Over the next hour, they opted out one at a time. With the control cabin gauge at thirty-five, they were all sealed up.

At fourteen hundred hours, Hobbs at the main scanner spoke on the general net. "There's something going on in Tregasid. Weekend migration by the look of it. Traffic building up on the throughways. All off towards the coast."

Crew not on watch had gravitated to the ward room where the ship's temperature control system was fighting a step-by-step rearguard. Conversation through suit intercoms had died the death. Each one was isolated in his own bulky shell.

Tamar Kelly said, "Leaving now, going by car to the coast, then by boat, they'd reach that island for Dusk 1. They must be holding one of their jamborees."

When it was out and said, echoing around the inside of her visor, she felt that in some way she was involved. She gathered her train of umbilical cords over her left arm and clumped off to her own cabin, a pachyderm withdrawing to a private sector of the forest to think a thing through.

She sat heavily on her acceleration couch and leaned on the bulkhead. Heat was notching up by small accretions. Clear thinking would be more difficult as the time ran on. Medoc was on a winner. Another two hours, perhaps less, and they would all be opting for out.

Eyes closed, she thought about Fletcher. She could see him walking away across the square, flat athletic back, head tall.

They had not had much time, but it was a breakthrough out of isolation. There was something in the theory that for every individual walking to and fro in the world there was a counterpart, and if the fantastic odds against meeting came out by good fortune on your side you were one of the favored few.

It had happened. She had the *entree* into his head. Words would never be very necessary between them. They were two of a kind.

She was drifting in and out of an uneasy sleep. Muddled sequences of Earth, Fingalna and Bromius itself were running through the holographic structure of her mind.

Then the stored fragments of past experience gave way to a section, vivid and immediate, which she knew for a truth was happening in the here and now.

She was experiencing the motion of a seagoing craft. There was the vibration through the hull of a propulsion pack, the rise and fall of the deck over a long swell.

She knew she was on a trimaran and the long curved cabin crossed three hulls with creaming bow waves. Dag Fletcher was lying on his back, ankles and wrists clipped to a tubular stretcher frame.

The pattern jelled. The boat was crossing one of the freak magnetic fields which lay off the island. Another ten minutes and it would be at the quayside.

Strangely enough she could only see Fletcher,

though there must be others present on the set. But the purpose was plain. He was destined for the knoll of infrangom at the end of the processional way.

Tamar Kelly saw her own cabin regroup itself around her head and was gasping for breath. She switched her suit to its last reading for heat control and the built-in powerpack began to whine with overload. Then she drove herself off the couch and went looking for Scullion.

He was turning slowly on the command island, a disillusioned man.

When she crossed to her own desk and began to work on the course data computer, he stopped circling and watched her in silence.

It was a long chore and she was still at it when he called all hands to the control cabin for the final showdown.

They came slowly. Holdbrook could barely move and dropped into his chair like a bulky zombie. Heat shimmer from the metal bulkheads was distorting vision and Scullion's voice was a gravelly whisper.

"I guess we all know that Medoc wins this one. It's just a question of whether I call him and agree to his terms or destroy the ship. A military unit would be expected to do just that. We are not a military unit and I'll take the majority opinion. But we should make it quick or we won't be able to form an intelligent opinion."

Hobb's voice was dry and cracked. "We can't help Fletcher and we can't help ourselves. There's no call for heroics. Tell him we'll meet him. Who knows, there could be a chance to get the information out. If we're all dead there's none."

Nobody else spoke. Scullion said, "Use your clearance signals. A green light agrees with that. A red says no."

There was a pause. Hobbs shoved over his "all systems go" lever and a green telltale glowed on the copilot's console. Holdbrook followed. Then Diggory Taft. Averil Marr was five seconds debating it and then the same.

Scullion said, "I have majority. What about you, Tamar, for the record?"

Tamar Kelly said, "It's agreed we can't leave the gravisphere because of the Scotian and we can't stay here. But there is a third angle. I've been working it out. On a low trajectory we can shift *Interstellar X* to another part of Bromius. It may only be a short-term gain, but I believe we should try it first. Look. That's the math of it."

She used the main scanner as a visual aid and began to talk it through in a husky monotone.

Dag Fletcher believed he was blind. Eyes open or closed saw only black. Tactile clues began to crowd his data acquisition network. He was lying face-down on a hard, smooth surface. His left leg was hooked in a stall some centimeters off the deck. There was a coolness in the air that had a free run along the length of his spine.

Orientation was rapid thereafter. Shifting over on his side, he could see the dark mass of a skyline separating out. Stars even. A pallor in the sky farther around. That would be the long quayside with its street-lighting system.

He was hooked up to the metal tree, naked as any needle and with a mouth like the bottom of a baby buggy, all ammonia and biscuit.

Movement dead ahead blocked his view of the night sky. It was a human silhouette growing darkly

193

from the ground. He got his weight balanced on two hands and his right foot and shoved off until he was standing upright back against the tree.

Sinclair in his own closed circuit of pain had not noticed the move and began cursing in a monotone. A chain rattled against the ground as he tried to free his leg.

Fletcher said, "Easy, Dave. Take it easy. ·Get yourself over this way. There's a bollard to lean on."

"Commander. God, I thought I was the only fool to be taken in by these twisty apes. They had me on an interrogation hookup. I guess they know all I know, but Christ knows that isn't much. Where's this then? What happens now?"

Sinclair could have used both feet for balance and had to hold on to the tree while the grove stopped its slow spin and stabilized.

A scuff of movement from the other side had Fletcher hopping around ready to grab. But the drag of a chain link told its own tale. It was one of the club. It must be Tamar. Bitterness flooded his mind. His blundering had gotten them all in this rats' alley. He should have followed Spencer's advice: made his inquiry for the record and taken *Interstellar X* out of it.

The voice coming from the gloom was on the deep side, though notched up a tone or two from its usual register, as Gary Wilson tripped over his tether and asked in simple rhetoric what was the name of the game they were playing at this point in time. Translated to his chilly plinth from the warm womb of the night spot without any intervening clue, he had every right to be puzzled.

Knowing him well, Sinclair was first with a recognition signal. He said, "Gary, you lecherous swine.

It's happened to you at last. You've been staked out for a goat. Follow your chain."

Relief that it was not Tamar was enough to keep Fletcher silent until the man was standing at his side. Then he said, "What's the score, Gary? How do you get to be here?"

"Commander. That's handy. I was sent out to contact you. There's trouble at the port. Two military units on the pad. Scullion reckoned it was time we pulled out and let I.G.O. work on the problem."

"Is Tamar Kelly on board?"

"Not when I left, chief. Though when that was I couldn't rightly say. I've had a very confusing sequence."

Sinclair said, "A confusing sexy sequence from what you were saying. Number one must be out of his head sending you on a search detail. Anybody would know where you'd start looking."

Wilson let it ride; he had enough to think about. "What's going on, commander? What are we here for?"

It was a seminal question that had been asked regularly through the millennia without anybody making a definitive answer. Taking its narrowest bearing, Fletcher said bluntly, "Variants of the priest king myth. Waiting to be sacrificed. This is where we see the other face of Bromius."

Having already seen it in part, Sinclair said, "God knows you wouldn't think there was anything but flowerlike charm, but I tell you that's a front. Alva had me sure I was her apple, but it was all an act."

Wilson said sententiously, "If you are an apple you have to endure the biting."

Over the rim of the oval clearing the long nimbus of light from the quayside had gathered a thin orange glow which thickened in a deepening V in its center, an illuminated pointer stabbing along the approach road to the grove.

Fletcher said, "Hold it." They listened. Above the slight noises of the wood there was a soft insistent drumbeat and a faint weaving line of melody from a woodwind section. "They're on their way. Stay back close to the tree. That way we have better balance and they have to come in close."

The V was a line now, at right angles to the assembly road, a broad orange mark creeping toward the tree like an illuminated strip in a flow diagram.

Massed human voices were taking up the rhythm, *largo* with the slap of feet in unison on the beat. It was an ululation starting low and cutting off abruptly in midflight. There was a quality about it which hit a harmonic in the mind. It was an aural drug. An exaltolide. By the time the multitude reached the grove the victims would be brain-washed into accepting their role, hopping out to the end of their chains to rush on immolation.

Fletcher said sharply, "Don't listen to that stench in the ear. Search around. There are free chains. Practice swinging one."

The wow of an iron cuff past his face had him putting in a hasty veto. "Not like that, Gary. Separate out around the tree. Take one-twenty degrees of arc. Sing a chantey to beat that rhythm."

Beating his brain for a tune he could only come up with "Nine Green Bottles", but it would serve as well as another and they roared it out as a counter-blast—Wilson, with an unsuspected flair, putting in a tricky descant.

Second time through with seven bottles still intact, the orange line hit the grove. Massed resin torches made the glare, packed solid in a broad river of flame, swaying and dipping, red glow on sweating faces.

The rhythm they were trying to beat had accelerated to a fast *adagio*, seventy-five to the minute reinforced by the slap of bare feet on the roadway.

The column split into two wings left and right, two turbulent rivers to circle the mound and surround the tree.

Mass hysteria was generating its own forcefield. Fletcher knew how it would be. It was in the very air. As soon as the circle was complete there would be a concerted overwhelming rush for the center.

Now the self-induced frenzy was an independent force acting outside any individual will.

As the two horns joined at the far side of the grove there was a single ecstatic yell and a new element flared into the composition. The long narrow axis which ran to the two circular terminals deep in the forest flicked into brilliant green light and two spots beamed out to center on the mound and its stark tree.

At the same time a red sphere lobbed itself over the skyline and moved slowly above the bright scar.

It was a recreation of the lost seventh moon of Bromius giving continuity to the ancient ceremony.

Small groups separated from the main mass of the people and began a jerky run towards the center. The combination of lights had a macabre effect on the pale white skins of the leading Bromusians, who were simply dressed in conical straw hats with small brims and narrow belts holding a *machete*.

There were nine in each party and at fifty meters it was plain that they were all young and all female. Two more leaping paces and they threw down their torches and drew their knives in a double grip.

With a concerted sobbing scream they rushed for

the mound, whirling the long blades in a figure eight that glittered in the spotlights as though it had been drawn by luminous paint in the air itself.

Behind them the crowd had closed in and gone silent. Only a single drum kept the rhythm of their bare feet as they started up the slope.

Fletcher swung his free chain across his front, recovered it and whipped it back the other way. Out of the tail of his eye he could see Sinclair doing the same.

He knew it was no good. Once it had hit he would be wide open until he could swing it again and there would be no time.

Sinclair's party was fractionally ahead and he could feel the jar transmitted by the tree at his back as the engineer caught the leader across the chest with his chain.

She was lifted off her feet and thrown back into the knife of the girl behind. She screamed once and again as the blade bit into the side of her neck.

Then Fletcher had his own battle joined. Sweeping the chain low, he caught two below the knee and brought them down in a tangle. Those pressing on behind checked long enough to stab the fallen before the knives were thrusting at him again.

They were insane for blood. Anybody's blood. He did his best to make it theirs, felt a sharp sear in his left side, felt the chain tangle and fall, reckoned that this was it. After all the long voyaging, he had reached the butt and seamark of his utmost sail. He looked up at the sky, the thoroughfare which had brought him to this omega point on his personal enterprise, and saw that the red moon was stationary over the tree.

It was a very subtle artifact indeed for a nontechnical people and gave full support for Medoc's claim that Bromius had forgotten more than most cultures had ever known.

Seen closer it was not round but polygonal, with every facet glowing like a jewel. It was bristling with delicate antennae. Maybe it had originally been designed as a research satellite.

The fact that he was still alive to sift the data suddenly registered. A blade held in a rigid arm was poised half a meter off his head, but the girl holding it was still as death looking up at the sky in a taut pose that stiffened her breasts into ivory tusks.

Wilson, better placed to see the action, croaked out, "Holy cow. It's the ship."

Dag Fletcher grabbed for her wrists and twisted the *machete* free. When he had it he swept around in an arc to clear a path. Then he edged towards Wilson to see for himself.

Interstellar X was falling in a fierce blast of retro towards the clearing.

Bromusians were trampling each other in a bid to get clear of the landing area. The drum had stopped.

The maenads at the knoll seemed to have taken it harder than most. Puppets with the strings dropped, they looked pathetic in their straw hats.

There was another twist for their occult gut. As the dark, falling spire of the ship leveled with the red moon a line of brilliant, eye-aching light ran between them.

The satellite sidestepped out of the sky, spinning crazily on its axis and went down in the bush between the grove and the long quay. An asterisk of vermilion flame marked the spot and the forest began to burn.

Interstellar X continued down, hit the pad, flexed on her jacks and shrouded herself briefly with coolant.

Out of the murk, the scout car arrowed in a direct line for the tree.

Fletcher, weary as death, was on his knees, leaning forward for support on the *machete* and looking on the carnage with a clouding eye. One way or another, he had seen it all before, but this was ramming home the point that there was never a straight edge in human terms. The proposition that the human mind would choose the good, the beautiful and the true when given an even chance was taking another knock.

Maybe it wasn't even true and if that was so he had wasted his time in I.G.O.

Bromius had been civilized for so long that the records ran out. But the skin of culture was still paper-thin and underneath was unregenerate Adam or in this case Eve, ready to short-circuit into savagery at the drop of a hat. Cultivating it even. Giving the ID a regular outing on schedule.

For that matter it was a phenomenon not restricted to Bromius. Everywhere civilization was dearly bought and insecurely held. Barbarism was nearer the surface than you would guess.

The scout car homed on the mound and two figures in white coveralls spilled out before the skids touched down. Diggory Taft had a service laser in either hand and covered his coworker who raced for the tree with a vibrator.

She reached Fletcher in a confusing blur and he was struggling to get to his feet to swing the *machete* in a last stand when she said, "It's the marines," and sliced through his irons with a neat economical action.

Calling over her shoulder, "Get to the car," she was off for the next in line.

He heard her say to Sinclair, "We ought to leave

you here, you big ape," and he found he was grinning at nothing in particular.

Pessimism was a dead duck. He had a ship and in that context he had work to do which was enough for the here and now.

As he came up, Taft said, "Are you OK, commander?" and Hobbs leaned out from the hatch to pull him aboard.

Moving slowly, smearing blood on the coaming, he heaved himself in as Wilson and Sinclair stumbled alongside.

The crowd in the clearing had recovered from the first shock. Random movement checked. They recognized that human intervention had disrupted the wake. There was a sudden rush for the mound as though they realized at the same split second that there was still a chance to turn back the clock.

Tamar was in, following Fletcher to the narrow freight bay and leaning over him, careless of all opinion to say, "Now I don't really care what happens as long as I'm with you."

Taft had a foot on the skid and a hand on a holdfast as Hobbs gave it the gun and the car accelerated away less than half a meter over the heads of the first wave to reach the mound.

From the direct vision port of the command cabin on *Interstellar X*, the island appeared to be ringed in flame. The latest ceremony in the long line had been a bonanza.

Fletcher, circling with Scullion at the dual desk on the command island, reckoned that survivors would need convincing that the ritual was a good idea.

Laced with an instant suture and topped up with plasma, he was feeling half a step out of key, but ready to hear the score. When Scullion had finished a quick outline, he believed that from a personal point of view it might have been just as well if he had let the virgin executioners do their thing.

Hobbs had the Scotian centered on the main scanner. The silver pencil was rock steady, overhead. She had shifted from her parking orbit over Thegasid to keep tabs on the Earth ship. It was a continuing mystery why her captain had held his hand so far.

Fletcher used his one-to-one link with his copilot. "You took a chance, number one, moving under that kitehawk. I'll not say we don't appreciate it, however."

"Any bouquets go to communications. Tamar worked it out and proved that we could do it. Anyway we couldn't stay on the pad. They were hitting us with a heat beam."

"So they really decided to come out in the open. That figures. But you weren't to know where we were."

"Tamar again. Personal radar working for you. I had a near mutiny, I'll tell you."

Switching to the general net, Fletcher said, "Communications. What's the picture? Can you transmit?"

Hobbs replied for the section. "Not a chance, commander. They've put the planet in a bag."

So it was back to square one. Anytime at all Medoc would cut his losses and give the Scotian the all clear to blast the Earth ship. It was the only logical step. He could not afford to let any one of them survive to tell the tale. He was not in a situation of his own choosing, but the sooner they were silenced the better.

Fletcher said, "Hear this. Time is running out. At some point their radio screen ends. We have to try to breach it. The Scotian goes by logic. He won't expect us to try the impossible. That might give us a few minutes before he realizes what we are doing. As soon as we move, I want a short message to go out on the intergalactic distress frequency code reference and 'under attack' will be all you can use. That will bring in the nearest task force and need some explaining away. Any questions?"

There was silence. It was only too clear.

"OK. Countdown as of now. I'll take her on manual. It's an academic point, but before we go, I have a log entry to make."

The sweep second hand was checking off the brief units to blastoff as he transferred rapidly to the recorder: "Starship *Interstellar X* commander's log. I have to record total satisfaction with the performance of all crew on this mission."

A rush of green telltales broke out on his console and he released the button. There was anyway nothing else to say. He shoved down the red lever that completed the firing cycle and cleared his mind of every other factor except the one overriding need to keep his ship in one piece long enough for the signal to get out.

Lurid flame beat around the grove and *Interstellar X* jacked herself over the treeline, arrow-straight for the waiting Scotian.

Fletcher forgot instrumentation. Working by the feel of it and listening to a cold countdown in his own head, he began to call for course changes that would have dropped a civilian ship back on its pad as a smoldering wreck.

They worked at it, giving him every fraction of concentration they had, nine brains working in one head.

A brilliant flare past the direct vision port told him that the Scotian had come off the fence.

The main scanner showed a whole new area of forest burst into instant inferno. *Interstellar X* shifted bodily off-course in the turbulence.

Fletcher had her over, filling the void as the Scotian corrected and fired again into the space they had just left.

It was impossible and they all knew it. But Holdbrook was pounding his console and fairly yelling. "The bastard. We'll do it yet."

Taft called from his module in the cone, "I have the range. Permission to open fire."

"Hold it." Fletcher wanted all the power they had. He flung the ship in a dizzy climbing spiral. His jury-rigged body tissue felt to be coming apart at the seams and he was biting the inner rim of his visor to damp down the pain. Light radiated the cabin and robot damage reporters sent a rush of red signals over the command console. But she was still clawing distance out of the sky.

Hobbs said urgently. "I have a channel."

The signal was repeated over the intercom. *"Interstellar X. Under attack Interstellar X. Under attack."*

Fletcher called the gunner in a harsh rasp. "Go ahead. Open fire."

It was a last gesture that the ship could make. Any second now the frigate's armament would lock on and they would not know. It would be quick, final, irrevocable, an instant translation to the majority group of the dead. There was time for a personal codicil and he thought of Tamar Kelly's shining head under the impersonal cowl of her visor and knew for a truth that his odyssey could have ended at that human island.

Then he was looking in simple disbelief at the scanner. The Scotian was breaking apart at her wasp waist, glowing incandescent, folding in on herself.

It was incredible that the old corvette's popgun armament could have done it.

Beyond it as it fell out of the sky there was another shape streaking forward with a brilliant lance of destruction still flaring from its fluted cone.

A new voice sounded from the communications desk: "Calling *Interstellar X*. You are requested to home on Tregasid spaceport. Do you require assistance?"

Fletcher said thickly, "Answer that, Mr. Scullion. Tell him to alert emergency services. But we'll be there. By God we'll get her there if we have to bale out and lower her by hand."

Then he was using every last kick of a failing motor to bring the ship on a new course.

When she dropped on her pad leaning five degrees off true on a buckled jack, he reckoned they had used up their ration of luck for a long lifetime.

Close by, another ship paced them in, filling the observation port with its silver bulk. Hobbs read the legend over her main hatch set in the blue-and-gold blazon of the I.G.O. military arm. *Europa*. He called on the general net. "That's service. Two calls and they drop out of a clear sky. You can't get better than that."

Fletcher's well of libido had run dry. He could not have raised a whistle for Aphrodite her own self drifting past the window on her scallop shell. His clips and the rigidity of his suit kept him erect at the command desk but black night filled his eyes.

First impression was that he had wakened out of season on his bier. He was stiff enough and there were flowers at all compass points. Maybe it was the next phase after ritual slaughter, and the Bromusians did the courteous thing by the corpse in the way of burial.

Sensors steadily working back to strength nine, he picked up a familiar scent from the left and twisted his head in its neck stall.

Tamar Kelly said, "Hi", in a pleased husky voice and leaned over his trundle bed.

It was on the short side for a communications expert. But her eyes, ten centimeters distant, were all the channel that he needed. They were wide and frank and making no reservations.

She said, "You'd like to know that it's all wrapped up. *Europa* came ahead of the squadron. Now they're all round the port. I.G.O. has put in an interim governing council. Medoc's agreed to put the infrangom into the strategic pool. There's a whole raft of money in it, so European Space gets full indemnity for all losses. So Spencer's pleased. We'll be a month refitting the ship. So we all have a leave. The Bromusians can't do enough for us. It should be a jig to remember."

Fletcher looked down his bandaged length.

"Not to worry. You'll be out of your straightjacket by tomorrow. All set to gather the nuts in May."

"Where shall we go?"

"I was hoping you'd ask that. I've been offered a sort of castle on one of the islands. I didn't say yes until you had the vote."

"Get this damned strapping off of my hands."

"It wouldn't be right. You'll just have to be patient. After all, it is said to be better to travel hopefully than to arrive. I'll go and tell that Bromusian to get the drawbridge down and shake the dust out of his arras."

Warm lips brushed briefly across his forehead and

she was out of range, hair swinging in an elastic bell.

But he was content. At a deep unreasoning level he was content. Rightly considered, the Bromius phenomenon was everywhere. Surface and inner purpose at odds. But not with Tamar. What she appeared to be, she was in truth.

After much beating about in the interstellar spaces he had reached anchorage in the eye of the wind.